THE LEAVETAKING

'*The Leavetaking* represents an achievement of a very high order and substantiates the belief that its author is among the half-dozen practising writers of English prose most worthy of attention' – *The Times Literary Supplement*

' . . . so sensitive, so deeply moving and so brilliantly written . . . a triumph which might well serve as a model for all young writers and, of course, a joy for all connoisseurs of fiction . . . it is the most sensitive as well as the most powerful portrayal of adolescence in modern Irish literature. One has to go back to Joyce to find anything to equal it . . . It is the work of a supremely gifted novelist' – *Hibernia*

ALSO BY JOHN McGAHERN

Nightlines
The Dark
The Barracks

THE LEAVETAKING

JOHN McGAHERN

QUARTET BOOKS LONDON, MELBOURNE,
NEW YORK

Published by Quartet Books Limited 1977
A member of the Namara Group
27 Goodge Street, London W1P 1FD
Reprinted 1977

First published by Faber & Faber Limited, London, 1974

ISBN 0 7043 3125 X

Printed in Great Britain by
Hunt Barnard Printing Ltd, Aylesbury, Bucks.

To Niall Walsh

Part One

I watch a gull's shadow float among feet on the concrete as I walk in a day of my life with a bell, its brass tongue in my hand, and think after all that the first constant was water.

Two boys drag a smaller boy towards me through the milling bodies. He is sobbing. I have to lean forward to hear in the din.

"He says Billy Rudge has been throwing pebbles at his glasses, sir."

"Tell Billy Rudge from me if it happens again he'll go to the office."

They run, gripping the small boy between them, who is smiling now behind the cheap misted spectacles. I hadn't to think to answer. After all the years on the concrete everything had become mechanical now, comforting hand on hair or warning tap on shoulder, the Red Cross kit in the office, telephone for the ambulance when limbs were broken.

I turn to watch the shadows float, calmly crossing and recrossing the milling shoes and hanging for moments still, how calm and graceful they float or hang still: the air above full of squawking gulls, clumsily turning, the hanging stilts of the claws and the bootbutton eyes tacked to the side of the skull as they wait for the abandoned scraps of bread.

"*Bhuil cead agan dul go dti an leithreas, a mhaistir*?" a boy asks my permission to go to the lavatory.

"Why didn't you go with your class when I rang the bell?"

"I forgot, sir."

"Do you really need to go?"

"Not really, sir," he grins and gallops away before I mechanically say, "Well why did you ask then?" and I do not call him back but follow a floating shadow again, the brass tongue of the bell warm in my hand; and I shiver, once it had seemed it would go on lunchtime after lunchtime as this until I withered into a pension at sixty-five, and yet today is the last day I'll walk with the bell. This evening he'll dismiss me when I meet him at eight. A smell of urine seeps from the lavatories, their small windows half open under the concrete eave.

The shadows sweep over the concrete, violent and very fast; and I search for one slow shadow to follow before turning to the air, where the violent sweep of the shadows is reflected in a white frenzy above as it nears to when they can fall on the scraps of bread.

I look on the shape of the buildings that on three sides enclose the concrete I walk on. The lavatories and schoolrooms are flatroofed and concrete, the single arm of the assembly hall alone v-roofed. Ragged rose bushes hang limp under its windows, a strip of black earth in concrete, the concrete beginning to crack after ten years, half-arsed modern as the rest of the country; the two halves of the yard slope in opposite directions. When it was first put down the plans had been read wrong and the slope had flooded the rains into the school, one half having to be torn up and sloped back towards the centre.

Across the low flat roofs of the schoolrooms I look towards the girls' school, a nineteenth-century mansion framed in beeches. The iron stairs of the fire escape climb to the door and window where the women lunch, low in the window black hair I kissed once, woman that I loved once: that love has gone and both of us live on though it seemed death then. Now that her power has gone she blushes when we meet, she who was indifferent to me or bored when she had power, as if she feels the part of her life that is gone has been enclosed by my love and could be recalled if the love could. She blushes now that part of her life is gone with the love, and still we live on.

Glass of the swing door glitters as it is pushed against the sunlight. It is Maloney, the headmaster, one hand outstretched as if in the dark to protect himself from the blind rushing of the play as he comes towards me across the concrete. The other hand mechanically draws itself from the forehead over his baldness: was it a habit he acquired in the horror of his early balding, drawing his palm over his hair in the hope that the hairs might miraculously cease coming away stuck to the sweat of the palm?

"*Go mba leithsceal, a mhaistir,*" he excuses as he reaches for the bell.

I let go the chain of the tongue when I feel the wood firmly in his hand; it tinkles before exploding into wild alarm and the yard freezes, the shadows floating very fast on the concrete as the gull cries enter the new silence when he holds the bell again by the tongue. A boy, unable to stand the tension of the awkward position he froze into at the bell, stumbles over laughing.

"You," he points the handle of the bell at the boy. "*Go dti an oifig*. No one moves after the bell stops."

As the boy makes his guilty way to the office the headmaster strides purposefully between the still figures, the shadows floating calmly on the concrete beneath the shrieking above. A gull drops low over one of the bins in an ungainly flap of wings but not close enough to pick the bread.

"When I give one ring to the bell each boy goes and picks up the lunchpaper nearest to him. Any boy I catch talking or not picking up papers goes to the office."

He changes his hand from the tongue to the handle and gives a single ring. The boys stoop to the concrete for the lunchpapers. "I said anybody I catch talking goes to the office," he adds as he hounds vigorously between the still figures in search of any papers left on the concrete.

"*Bhfuil gach duine ag eisteacht?* When I ring the bell again, walk with the papers to the bins and then quietly back to your places. Anybody running or talking goes to the office."

One sharp bell stroke. They walk to the bins. A medley of strikes tells them they can play again. They burst into relieved uproar, their feet threshing over the shadows that had floated in stillness. The point of the cane makes a ragged lump in the shoulder of his brown suit as he comes towards me with the bell, its yellow crook inside the silver watchstrap between his cuff and sleeve. As I take the bell by the tongue, shock of the erection I got when first I beat a boy with a cane, taking pleasure in my supposed duty. There is as much contained satisfaction on his face as he hands me the bell as Napoleon's must have worn after a perfectly executed cavalry manoeuvre.

"In about six minutes you can ring them up, *a mhaistir*," he says looking at his watch below the crook of the cane.

"*Gura maith agat, a mhaistir*," I prefer to thank him in the patriotic and official idiom since in it I am unable to betray shades of feeling.

"*Gura mile maith agat, a mhaistir*," he is elaborately polite today as he strokes his hand over his bald head and turns away. Normally he'd hang about with me on the concrete, "Who do you fancy for the next All Ireland?" or "Have you been down home lately?" or "What do you think of this new maths?" and I, having no strong opinion, would trot out, "I suppose they're all right, but I don't see how you can escape the hard slog—though they may be all right for the very clever," since I'd know it would please him.

"That's what I say. There's no escaping the basics. Those theories are all very fine to have behind a desk in Marlborough Street when you don't have to put them into practice. They sound good. You'll find no matter what theories you have there's no substitute for the hard slog. If they left teaching to teachers it'd be a saner world."

That would be the normal but normally the teacher on playground duty is not normally due to be dismissed at eight of the same day.

"Old fanatical peasant I'll miss you," I think as I watch him go towards the teachers' room, ready to rout them out of any argument into the playground at the first stroke of the bell, a little stooping as he goes, the bulge of the cane in the shoulder, obsessively stroking the bald head. He gives the same narrow care to this school as his father must have given to the crops and cattle of their small southern farm, "This school is me. I'll go through stone walls for this school."

Through the modern glass of the swing door I see him withdraw the cane from his sleeve, the tensed body of the boy as he holds out his hand for the cane, the single blow; and the boy crushing his folded arms in pain as he is propelled out through the swing door by the shoulder.

He's changed little from the first time we met, more than nine years before, a wet Saturday night a week before Christmas, the bus queues long with children and shoppers in Abbey Street, tired and irritable in the rain, the wind from the sea rocking the wall of the bus as it dropped me past the Bull. I was an hour early for the interview but the night was too wet to hang about the suburban avenues, their stripped almond and cherry waving under the lamps.

"I am sorry I am too early. I misjudged the time with the buses and it is wet."

He stood in the door no different than he stood today on the concrete, in one of the identical brown or blue suits, brown or black pairs of shoes.

"It makes no difference at all. You're welcome. I am sorry you've had such a bad night to come."

He took my coat and showed me into a front room, bustling as he turned on an electric fire, moving the heavy armchairs. The room was obviously little used by the family. A heavy clock, with the day of his wedding and the names of its donors on a silver scroll, beat on the fleshcoloured tiles of the low mantel.

"You'll have to excuse me. Mrs. Maloney is at Confessions, it's the Women's Sodality, and I have to try to get these troops you hear upstairs to bed before she comes."

"It's fine," I answered awkwardly as running feet and shouts sounded from the upstairs rooms.

I sat in the empty sittingroom, its white sliding doors closed, and listened to him try to get his children to bed with a mixture of not very effective bribes and vague threats. Later I was to come to know he had as little authority in his home as he had complete authority at school.

When he came I noticed for the first time his habit of drawing his hand across his head in the memory of hair as ruefully he smiled, "Always it's a struggle. That's what you'll have ahead of you on Sodality nights when you're married."

Solicitously he moved the electric fire closer before taking my letter of application from the top of a piano in the bay of the window.

"I liked your application and especially how both inspectors stress your *modh-briomhar* in both your probationary reports. If a young teacher hasn't energy and ethusiasm he might as well throw his hat at it."

"I am happy where I teach now," I lied with measured falseness. I hated the small town where I then taught and wanted to get to the anonymity of the city at any cost, "But the journey and the fares to the university in the evenings I am finding a struggle."

I had started night lectures as excuse to escape the dreariness of the evenings of the small town, dreariness of the digs I shared with four artificial inseminators.

"I'm the oldest. If I could move to the city it'd be to help more with the younger children's education," I lied on, the lies like all successful lying compounded of an element of truth.

"Actually, my wife remarked on that in your application. It's an old country tradition. The first out of the nest helps the others out. City people are all right in their way but they don't have those good solid traditions behind them that we who come from the country have."

The white sliding doors parted slowly to show a small boy in pink nightwear who shouted, "Cuckoo, Daddy," and stood there smiling.

"Gerald, such manners," he rose. "You know you shouldn't have got out of bed. You'll have to excuse me again," but the child scampered back into the darkness behind the sliding doors and it took some time before he was able to catch him and carry him kicking happily upstairs again to his bed.

"When you have children of your own you'll realize how simple and uncomplicated your life is now," he stroked his hand ruefully over his head when he came down but before he had time to return to the application a key turned in the door.

"Thank God, it's Mrs. Maloney back from the Sodality," he went and called her into the room as she was putting away raincoat and umbrella in the hall.

"She was a teacher too before we were married. Not far from your part of the country."

"My mother taught in Leitrim too before she died."

"My father must have known her then. He was principal in Lecarrow," she said smiling, a large woman, with warm brown eyes, her black hair threaded with grey, the irregular features welded into one impression of solidity and warmth, more handsome now than probably ever she was when young. I named my mother's maiden name.

"Of course," she answered. "I often heard my father speak of her. Nobody had anything but praise for your mother."

The interview was over. I had got the job. The headmaster beamed, it was all he needed to be certain, he was now appointing someone from within the family, not taking a chance on a mere stranger.

"When you've had a look at those heartscalds upstairs why don't we all have tea in here," he said to his wife.

"Have they been playacting again on you?" she laughed lightly.

"They never stopped. Nothing I say in this house is paid any attention to," he grimaced wryly. "Their behaviour must have made a terrible first impression."

"They are only children after all," I answered awkwardly.

"Still, we'd not have behaved like that with *our* parents. We walked around in fear," and he began to tell me about his father, a small southern farmer, a quiet man but hard, who slaved from light to dark to give them an education and a chance in life that he himself had never had. People come by things too easily nowadays, he thought.

Tea and biscuits and fruitcake she brought in on a tray. Talk went as the slow dropping of rounded stones from jar into separate jar. I did not ask till it was time to leave, "Do you think have I chance of the appointment?"

"I can't appoint you. Father Curry is the Manager. He does the appointing, but in all the years he's never once gone against my recommendation, though of course the final say is his," he more smiled than grinned, an old servant smiling with loving indulgence on the gods of authority since in spite of all their power they were as small children in his hands once he had learned how to humour their little ways. "He says twelve Mass in St. Anthony's on the seafront tomorrow. Meet me at the gates at half-twelve tomorrow and we'll see what we can do."

We met at the chapel gate, the rain had stopped, sun coming and going behind white cloud out on the bay.

"It'll be longer than I thought because of benediction. We might as well wait inside," he said and I was glad to avoid the unease of waiting alone together.

In the porch two men were counting coins into blue paper-bags on the table and they nodded friendly recognition to the headmaster. "They're parents of some of our pupils," he leaned to whisper as we went in. "Great parishioners. I'll tell you about them later."

We stood together at the back of the congregation; above us the choir was singing, the air warm and heavy with incense and bodies. A bell tinkled. In silence the little fat old priest climbed toward the tabernacle. The monstrance glittered a metallic sun as he moved it in the shape of the cross before downcast eyes. The bell tinkled for a last time into the shrouded coughing, into some child's crying, and it was soon over, the altar boys in scarlet and white leaving the altar in twos in front of the priest bearing the empty monstrance, light from candles dancing on the gold of his cloak, small human bundle in magnificent clothes. In the sacristy they would be free of the mystery when the boys bowed with the priest to the cross and then to one another, as I did too when I was young.

We were pushed by the surge towards the doors out again to the gates to wait, the congregation scattering to cars and bus queues or just walking away as a huge handful of feathers scattered on a stream.

"You stand a little way off. I'll see what mood he's in first. If he's in the right mood I'll beckon you over. If not I won't. We'll leave it as it is if he's grumpy until a better time."

Pausing steps came at last from the sacristy, the small rosy corpulence in black, the headmaster moving nervously along on the railing, searching for the best position to effect the meeting.

"My friend," the priest raised a short arm to the headmaster's stooping shoulder. "It was just yourself I was wanting to see," and they sauntered out of earshot, stopping some yards off with the priest deep in earnest speech.

It was some time before I was beckoned over.

"I'm glad to meet you," he held out a warm pudge of a hand. "And what part of the country are you from?"

"Leitrim, Father."

"There was a Flanagan from Leitrim in my class in Rome."

"He might be from another part of the county, Father."

"Anyhow, it'd be before your time and I somehow remember hearing the family had moved. He was an excellent handballer."

Maloney leaned above the conversation, beaming approval, waiting for the right pause to interject, "I am hoping, with your approval, Father, that Mr. Moran will prove a fine addition to St. Christopher's."

"You're not long out of the College?" he felt it necessary to go through a semblance of an interrogation.

"Two years, Father."

"And I suppose his reports are good?" he turned to the headmaster.

"Excellent, Father. They stress enthusiasm and energy."

"What about an interest in games?"

"I'd be glad to help at games."

"That's better than a hundred reports. *Mens sana in corpore sano,* I always say. Better than a hundred highfaluting theories. Some of those highfaluting theologians who used to lecture us in Rome I'd give my right arm to see them try and run an honest parish."

"Perhaps you'd like some time to think over the appointment, Father?" Maloney decided to intervene.

"No, if you think he's all right that's that. You're welcome among us," he shook my hand. "You're coming to the best school in Dublin and the best headmaster."

He let go my hand, changing his to the headmaster's arm, "It's an infernal nuisance having to go to court with that bowsie of a contractor Ryan. After him putting down the concrete so that the water flooded the school he has the impertinence to get his solicitor to write that I was to blame."

I watched them drift slowly as in the beginning along the railing, the priest talking, the headmaster's body bent low and nodding obsequiously until they reached the presbytery gate where the priest took his leave by a squeeze of the arm.

"That's a good morning's work," the headmaster rubbed his hands in satisfaction when he came back. "He's as good a Manager as a school could have as long as you never press him when he's in the wrong mood."

"He has agreed to the appointment then?"

"There was no trouble. What he wanted to talk about was a court action that's coming up over the playground. It was sloped the wrong way so that the water flooded the school. Between myself and yourself and the wall he'll have to cough up but you couldn't tell him that. He left it all to a lazy clerk-of-works that someone pawned off on him."

"Should we have a drink to celebrate?" I asked and his face fell: fear that he'd just hired a drunkard. His finger searched to his lapel, "I must have left my pin in the other suit," he explained in confusion.

"I didn't mean in a pub," I quickly corrected. "An orange or lemonade in a sweet shop."

"That's an idea," he relaxed in relief.

We passed The Yacht as if it was a house of shame.

"Young teachers should stay clear of the pub. There can be too much free time in the profession. I've seen too many in my day come to grief on the high stool," he advised as we reached a sweet shop and stood for a few minutes beside a pile of Sunday papers drinking from lemonade bottles through pale straws, but my appointment was now secure. It was all of nine years ago.

At one minute to one today as on every other schoolday, leaving the door of the staffroom open on the teachers, he'll come through the swing door on to the concrete.

I watch the shadows race over the milling boots, their bread is near, as I walk for the last time with the bell, its brass tongue in my hand.

I look at my watch as I see the headmaster hurry from the staffroom to his office, leaving the door open behind him: it is two minutes to one. I take the bell by the handle, the chain and ball tinkling as it falls free, and the yard freezes as I ring.

"Anybody moving after the bell goes straight to the office," the headmaster is outside the swing door, shouting into the voracious shrieking of the gulls. The second bell drowns his voice. They run to their lines. "No talking after the bell," I hear him shout as some murmur rises into the gull shriek.

"*Lamha suas*," I say and the lines stretch out as they put hands on each other's shoulders. "*Lamha sios*," their hands slap their sides.

"*Lamha sios*."

"*Lamha suas*."

"*Iompaigi*," for the last time and they turn, the headmaster moving among the lines as some brownsuited cormorant scanning water.

"Anybody who has something to give up can now leave his line."

"Black glove, rosary beads, medal," he names them as he holds them high. "Penknife. I'm giving it back but it's the last time. Knives should *not* be taken to school," he looks impatiently towards the open staffroom door. "Black glove, white handkerchief, rosary beads."

Boland is first in the doorway, but hangs back against the wall to take a few last guilty drags of the cigarette he holds behind his back, fifty-five-year-old schoolboy with heart condition, and so the shy and conscientious James is first on the concrete.

"Mr. James's class. March. *Cle, deas, cle,*" the headmaster at once sends the line moving towards the classroom, apologizing as James hurries past him to catch up with his class. "It's only just to get them moving, *Nil aon deifir, a mhaistir.*" "*Gura maith agat, a mhaistir,*" the quiet James thanks him as he goes past to catch his class. "*Cle, deas, cle, deas,*" James takes up to try to concentrate the life he feels haemorrhaging under the headmaster's eye until he can get to the quiet of his classroom, where he'll try to restore his loss of self with a silent curse before making the class stand for prayer before work, the work he'll do scrupulously and well.

Raggedly they are on the concrete now, my colleagues until eight this evening, Boland hanging farther back for the last guilty drags; and is there need to name them, soon they'll be only an impression they made on my mind, yellowing papers tied with weakening twine, no blue or pink loveknots to charm away the harshness. They have mortgages to pay off. They are worn out at the end of every June and come back vaguely reconditioned each September after breathing the sea of Dollymount if they cannot afford a change of sea. They let healing clay trickle through their fingers in small gardens that end with some young apple trees and a wall of concrete blocks topped with glass. They lean on spades across privet in the evenings and talk with their neighbours of the gardens and the road and in spite of the bills and the children's quarrels that can drag them into neighbouring quarrels, by September they will be partially healed.

The gulls' shadows race and whirl in a frenzy over the bread exposed on the concrete, only the bolder swooping low enough to lift the crust that they have then desperately to defend again in the air.

"*Rang a tri! Cle, deas, cle, deas,*" O'Connor claps his hands before the headmaster has time to set his class moving in advance. The class smile cockily toward him as they march. "*Rang a tri.* Brisk. March," he claps and they smile again, the clay of the young flesh reflecting their master's character. "*Cle, deas, cle, deas,*" he claps and as he passes the headmaster a jaunty, "Nice bit of sun for a change, *a mhaistir,*" and Maloney jostled for the moment out of his authority reacts in distracted confusion, "*Go haluinn buiochas le dia, a mhaistir,*" before returning to the concentration of a gundog pointed towards sleeping game as he watches the lines.

The shadows race and wheel and clash on the empty spaces, shrieking as they come down for the bread.

"*Rang a ceathar.* March," Jones, a little cock, says quietly and firmly to his line. Ramrod straight, razor of a crease from shining shoes, gold pin in the tie, white cuff. The grey hair shines from brushing.

"*Dia dhuit, a mhaistir,*" he says formally as a general saluting another general. "*Dia is murie dhuit, a mhaistir,*" the headmaster returns without looking up, intent on keeping the lines flowing towards the rooms so that no classroom time is wasted. He does not follow Jones's precise walk from the yard.

It is the last day and it is same as all the other days on the concrete, and it will go same as this after I am gone with only change of cast or of weather.

All the teachers are on the concrete except Boland who still hangs back for the last drags. The classes stream in a continuous line towards the open doors of the room. "*Cle, deas, cle . . . cle . . . cle,*" thumped out to the march of boots on the concrete. It is the last time? What do I take away? Not much, and it tells as much about me as them.

An engagement ring Doherty worked eighteen hours a day the whole summer in a pea canning factory near Newcastle to buy. "She will never know how much sleeplessness and sweat and lifesickness of green she wears on her pretty finger."

Such small confidences I'll take away.

"Did you feel like running?" O'Connor had asked him after he'd come from seeing his firstborn.

The blackhaired Tonroy who passes me now in rigid disapproval took me to his house once, "When we first met I'd to borrow sixpence from the sister to take her to the pictures and then I said get on your bike, girl, from now on for you're going out now with one of the impoverished brotherhood." Impoverishment of their house of children, not poverty but the ugly coldness that nothing—neither chair nor plate nor child—had ever been touched with care, the runny nose of a child. O the opposite of my love in the room in Howth, the love of the Other that with constant difficulty extends its care to all the things about her so that they shine in their own loveliness back to her as the circle closes in the calmness of the completed self, the love that I'll be fired from this school for at eight.

"*Cle; deas, cle . . .*"

O'Toole smiles at me as he goes past, at least he does not judge. They blame him for not being married, for taking the transistor to school in summer to listen to the cricket; they'd blame him anyhow, they need to blame.

Munroe is the one teacher to go up to the headmaster, who folds his arms and smiles as he listens to some tale of what happened at the church choir. Munroe's laughter peals out through buck teeth when he finishes; the headmaster smiles, but his eyes follow the marching feet, stirring uncomfortably if he sees any child out of line, "The time to nip it is in the bud, before it gets out of hand." Munroe waves as he finishes and hurries after his already marching class, he is the headmaster's right hand, they both live for the school.

I tighten my hand on the tongue of the bell to hand to the headmaster a last time, three lines left on the concrete, one of them beginning to march, I turn to the feel of Boland's hand on my shoulder.

"It's the best thing that ever happened to you. There's nothing I'm more sorry for than that they didn't sack me before I got too old, since I kept putting off taking the plunge till it got too late. One of my class that got sacked—roaring drunk he was on the job—is now head traveller for a chemical company, rolling in money, driving round the country from hotel to first-class hotel. His nerves aren't in tatters at the end of the day. The best thing ever happened to you. You'll get out before the trap closes."

"I hope you're right and thanks," I try to smile, I've always liked him and yet he makes me always awkward.

"Do you see these?" he takes his hand from my shoulder to show me photos. "I was showing them to the boys at lunch and it was too much of an eyeful for some of the sober joes. We took them on the Isle of Man in August." The photos are of a beauty contest, girls in swim-suits and high heels on a wooden platform against a pavilion and the sea. Under the platform Boland is prominent in dark glasses and a flowered shirt.

"You managed to get near enough to the lovelies," I say.

"Where would you expect me to be but near? We had a few bets on the result. I got the winner at four to one. A right boozeup we had afterwards in the Oak Lounge on the proceeds."

The third class had passed through the glass doors at the lavatory. Only my line and Boland's are left on the concrete. Maloney casts us glances as he paces between the lines. Many of the gulls have come down on the concrete, the shadows of those above dulling their white brightness in the moment of passing.

"I think Maloney is getting restless," I am anxious for him to leave. My class has to be last to leave after the handing over of the bell.

"That old bollocks. What do you care? You can't be sacked twice the same day anyhow. I wonder what he'd do if one of those dames waltzed up to him and took him by the fly. O my God how he managed ten children I'll never know. I'd give a week's wages to see him perform. The first five steps of the *modh-muinte*."

The headmaster soon lost patience.

"Mr. Boland's class. *Cle, deas, cle. Gluasaigi,*" rings out in the gull chatter and shriek.

"The old bollocks," Boland mutters as he leaves, "I'll show him the photos just for the crack. Remember what I told you though—this day'll be the best thing ever happened to you."

I turn towards the swing door to hide amusement from my class, who are watching me for word to *March*, as he flourishes up to the headmaster with the photos. I watch out of a corner of my eye. A thin smile surfaces to Maloney's features as he looks through the photos, the manner that of a policeman accosted by an amiable drunk, prepared to humour him a moment in order to hurry him the more quietly on his way. As he goes he waves a bragging arm to me behind the headmaster's back, fifty-five-year-old schoolboy with heart condition still at school, "*Cle, deas, cle,*" he shouts, and I hand over the bell.

"*Gura mile maith agat, a mhaistir,*" he thanks me. Normally, he might mention some point of playground discipline but today is, after all, a last handing over of the bell, by chain and tongue.

"*Gura maith agat, a mhaistir,*" I return, and call to my line to march. He walks towards the swing door, head low, slowly passing his hand backwards over his head, the bell hanging silent by its chain in his other hand; sad he is or reflective I think as I watch him leave, as if he was going over my life at the school and its ending or over his own life or all of life.

Grey gullshit falls close to me on the concrete as I walk by the side of my class towards the door by the lavatory. *Cle, deas, cle ... cle.* The shadows float and hang still on the concrete but they are thinning, drifting over the trees in the direction of Dollymount strand and the Bull, from where the autumnal smell of dying seaweed reaches me through the fresh urine. The concrete is clean of bread. The bootbutton eyes of the last gulls dispute a scrap of white loaf with claws and shrieking beaks, their shadows contracted to a small area of the concrete. When they leave for the sea the concrete will be empty of shadow, lying still and grey, reflecting its own light, as the first dog starts to scavenge among the bins. Over them the nineteenth-century house that is now the girls' school where the one with black hair teaches, whom I loved once; and now that love is changed, embodied around fair hair in a room in Howth. If I could pray I would that she be the last embodiment of love in my passing.

I follow the last child through the door at the lavatory. *Cle, deas cle ... cle.* Their shoes echo up the long empty corridor towards the one remaining open door of the classrooms near its end.

We chant the prayer before work. They take out their books. Mechanically I begin the lesson of the afternoon but I have no desire to bend to its arid discipline today of all days, if indeed I ever had. I'd never have been a teacher, I see clearly, but for my mother. Her dead world comes to life in my mind as I drift away from the classroom and out of this last day in it on a tide of memory.

"Who do you love most in the world?" my mother used often ask me in the evenings.

"You, mother," I answered her in that dead June evening.

"That's not right. You know who you love most."

"You, my mother."

The grey tassel of the blind swung to the idle touch of my hand in the window where I sat. A cinder path ran to the railway sleeper that made a footplank into the ripe June meadow outside, green and a leaden silver where it leaned in heavy ripeness, above it the black clouds of a gathering storm.

"No, this has gone far enough. You know who you must love most of all."

"I am lucky to have such a lovely mother to love," the tassel brushed the glass as I moved it faster.

"Enough fooling. You know *Who* your first love must be."

Her face lay in its pile of chestnut hair on the pillow. I let the tassel hang free. To get her love I'd have to trot out the catechism answers that I hated.

"God," I said.
"And after God?"
"Mary my Mother in Heaven."
"And after Mary?"
"You, mother."
"No. You know that's wrong."
"I love my earthly mother and father and brother and sisters equally," I resented then having to affirm what I did not feel.
"And after this life if we serve God well?"
"We'll live forever and forever with God in heaven."
I had no love for forever and forever in heaven, solemn song and music forever under evergreens to figures on burnished thrones in the higher distance, their white robes flowing. At best it might be Lenehan's orchard on a true summer's day: gravelled avenue climbing between laurel, the Virginia creeper below the turrets of the Bawn a rude riot of sparrows, white benches on the lawn, the band thumping out a samba from the marquee down by the river during summer carnival, carts rocking from the meadows and she and I together under a red and yellow canopy of apples and talking of our life in the world.
"We'll live happily forever and forever if we pray," she said from the pillow.
I let the tassel hang limp in the window. A dark green stillness had settled on the meadow. The sky was full of thunder.
"I'm afraid it's going to thunder, mother."
"You can come to me if it does."
The first crash trembled the thin walls of the house. An explosion of light on the widowpane and on the glass of the picture of the Sacred Heart above the wardrobe in the gloom. I ran to the bed.
"Hide me, O hide me, I don't want to go to hell."
She held me close to her on the bedclothes. With each survived crash I grew quieter.
"You wouldn't go to hell anyhow. And you're safe now.

Listen. It's moving away."

"I don't want to die. I want to stay with you."

"You won't die and it's moving away. You can count between the clap and flash. It's a mile away for every second you can count."

She began to count slowly from the next clap. She'd reached seven when the lightning flashed, "You see it's moved seven miles away." The thunder came again. Gently she led me through the counting. We reached ten before the room lit, "You see it's now ten miles away. You must count yourself the next time. It has nothing to do with hell."

I reached fourteen between the next rumble and its lightning.

"You counted a little fast but you can see it has moved further off still."

"We won't die so and go to hell, mother?"

"Not if we pray and fear God."

Heavy rain had started to drum on the slates, drumming anxiety and fear away in its fierce beat, it was suddenly happiness to be close to her on the bed under the roof and not outside in the pouring rain.

"What'll you be when you grow up?" it was a dream she recurrently loved to linger on.

"A priest, mother," my answer never changed.

"Do you think when you get older you may change your mind and want to be something different?"

"No. It's too hard to get to heaven if you're not a priest." It was said with that grave solemnity of children that moves the grown to smile.

"I am not a priest or a nun and I have to hope to go to heaven," she stroked my hair.

"That's different. You're a good person."

"I'll be present at your ordination, won't I?"

"I'll send a big car for you to come to Maynooth to see me ordained."

The dream never changed. She would go in a black car to my ordination. It would have no white ribbons or virginal flowers but it would be fulfilment of her wedding day. She'd kneel for the first blessing from my priest's hands when they'd taken the bandages off, hands fragrant with sweet oils.

She'd come with me to my first parish, to live in an old ivy-covered presbytery, a walk of white gravel through the cemetery between the church and the presbytery, an apple garden with some plum and ornamental fuchsia at the back. In moonlit nights the gravestones would shine white but they'd hold no terror for us. Grandfather clocks would strike the hours. Summers we'd read on the lawn and as the summer went watch the red fall of rose petals on its margins. She'd keep the altar, take the Dutch tulips from their thin cardboard boxes, arrange flowers and candles on the altar, be the constant worshipper and communicant at daily Mass.

"I'll say Masses for you when you're dead."

"You'll say Masses for me when I'm dead," she repeated with a catch of the breath.

"Lots and lots of Masses for you. You'll hardly have to spend any time at all in purgatory with all the Masses."

"You promise to say Mass for me?"

"I promise. And afterwards we'll live forever together in heaven."

"Kiss me," she raised her lips from the pillow. "It makes me so happy that one day you'll say Mass for me. You don't mind now if I try to sleep."

As she closed her eyes her face was full of a calm sweetness.

In the schoolroom of this day I am disgusted at the memory. Though who am I to judge or to expect her frail person to break the link against the need of the chain to lengthen and grow strong in normal darkness.

"You sent for me, mother?" her sickroom is more vivid in my mind than this classroom where I teach out the last day.

"Come over and sit on the bed. There's a draught between the door and window."

I moved to the bed's edge. The new eiderdown had black squares and red.

"Do you want me for something, mother?"

"I want you to promise to do what I am about to ask you."

"Promise what?"

"Just to promise me without asking what."

"I can't promise without knowing."

"Why do you have to be as Thomas who had to put his hand in the spear wound?"

"What do you want me to promise?"

"I want you to promise not to cry if I have to go away."

The face on the pillow of hair was grey but it looked a girl's face. The pale blue of the eyes held a paler pleading smile.

"For how long?" I barely was able to get the words out. She'd been away for months in hospital before. We'd to move to our father in the barracks. The hostile stone rooms of the barracks had been as nothing compared to the ache of waiting for her to come home. I flinched at the memory of the wild happiness of seeing her get out of the car at the end of the avenue the day the pheasant was shot for her, the world holding its breath a moment as the small figure in the grey tweed costume got out of the car at the end of the avenue. Silver fountain pencils with three pellets, red and green and yellow in its glass top were the thin wafers of communion she brought, a promise that she'd come home never to go away again.

"You must promise me not to cry?"

Even if I'd wanted to promise I could not.

"If I had to go away forever would you promise not to cry for me?"

"Why'd you have to go?" I gripped her arm.

"If God called me."

"No, no," I broke down, more against the horrible *To Die* trying to break into my mind out of her phrase, "If God called me."

Healing rage grew, the unfairness of it all.

God had all the angels and saints in heaven and his own mother, and why should he call the one and the only one I loved, all that I had.

Cheap plywood wardrobe of that room. Sprayed gold handle, Sacred Heart lamp burning before the Sacred Heart, window on the empty meadow, more present than this schoolroom where I stand and watch.

"Promise me, promise me you can't go," I shook the frail blades of her shoulders.

"I'll not go then. I promise. Not to go. Will that quiet you now?" Her face showed the despair of not being able to share her approaching death with me.

"It's certain?"

"It's certain. I promise not to go."

"It'll be summer soon, you'll be better, we'll go to town on the train, I'll carry the parcels . . ."

"I'll sleep a little now," she turned on her side away from the window. I stared at the bedclothes, shaken by small regular convulsions. She was probably sobbing but I did not know that then. The tassel hung still in the centre of the window. The meadow was bare beyond the railway sleeper, water glittering from hooftracks as stars in the worn grass. Raindrops spattered the pane, clung there a moment as if waiting to be told their purpose, but not having the strength to wait any longer for answer suddenly wasted down the glass.

I went past the window, looking back at the door but the face was hidden, the convulsions weaker in the bedclothes.

Bare boards of the corridor, loose brass knobs of the doors; shoes on the stairs, hand on its wooden railing, relief I had the cows to tie out in the darkening evening.

In the darkness of the byre they stood munching by their posts. I slipped their chains about their necks and hooked them shut. At the last cow, the old grey, as I hooked her chain I buried my face against her hair and warm flesh and started to cry.

Lightfoot, not my friend since he found friendship disgusting, quoting Proust that it is the halfway house between physical exhaustion and mental boredom. Only what one loves *is*, as we comically try to hang on to what must pass, and I respect

Lightfoot too much to claim him for a friend against his will. The simple feeling that such as he is alive is enough to make my own life more bearable and he made that wet evening in the deathroom general for me when he spoke of his own mother. We sat at the long marble counter of The Stag's Head, the silver clock on the slender stem crowned with antlers and the scroll of *tempus fugit*.

"She devoured her wretch of a husband my father and all my brothers except Tom who left the house at eighteen and would have nothing more to do with her. She still hates to mention his name. All the brothers that married are in turn dominated by their wives. Poor Kevin, who stayed in the house, she tramples all over; he takes her weekends in the country, he's fifty, and she butters his bread. She halfdevoured me and would have wholly except for me developing some awareness of it."

"She's always been charming to me," it was a question rather than a defence.

"That charm covers steel and I often think it comes from the mountains; all her people come from the mountains."

"I couldn't imagine her violent," I questioned again.

"No. That's why it is so deadly. She did it the way women do: a withdrawal of support at crucial moments. As they can enslave by the giving and refusal of sex."

It was not my story. My mother had no choice in her withdrawal, and yet Lightfoot's story that evening was a lamp, drawing the act out of its isolated darkness into recognition and odd comfort that life in different ways dealt the small deaths as pitilessly to everybody in preparation for the last. As I left him to go down the lane to the buses, the click of billiard balls coming as on this time every Saturday night from the Union Hall, I shivered in the face of a premonition of what I did not want to look on.

The day after she'd promised me not to die I remember going to visit my cousin Bridget. My feet stretch from sleeper to sleeper, sharp white stones between the sleepers, the two silver strips of the rail flashing as they narrow into the stone bridge. There is no cloud. I am purely happy going up the railway in the morning to visit my cousin Bridget. To add to my delight she is alone in the room, wrapping fresh bread in a damp towel for it to cool. The men would drive the ploughing horses, pitch high the sheaves, stick the pigs and sheep but at the centre of the farm the cave of this room would always be still, rich in bread and honey and steam, washed flagstones and bare wood of the table and chairs and the rounded ripeness of her young body.

"How is your mother?" I was disappointed that she did not give me her first attention.

"She's still in bed."

I hated having to think back to the tension of the house, I had wanted all this morning to myself, in the cave full of the fresh smell of bread, alone with Bridget Kiernan.

She put a steaming brown teapot on the table, a crate of honey in its wax on a big plate, and slices of brown bread on which the butter melted.

"I found this penny on the track," I showed, looking for her attention back.

"It's not money though anymore," she examined; the wheels of the train had pressed flat the impression of both the harp and the hen with chickens on the copper. "They won't take it in the shop. Your mother is long sick now?" I winced as she changed back.

"Since before Christmas."

"What do you think has her sick?"

"That wetting she got when she went on the bicycles to get the priest to sign the salary forms before Christmas."

"How do you know?"

"I went with her. It got dark in the rain after school."

"You didn't get sick from the rain?"

"No," I resentfully sipped the tea, this was not the lovely morning I had come for.

"Your mother didn't look very well to me when I was over to see her last week."

"She has two nurses now though," the peace had already gone.

"Say if she doesn't get better what'll you do?"

It was unimaginable that she would not get better but why was she talking so when I had come to enjoy with her the peace of the morning.

"She can't be much longer in bed. She has the two nurses."

"You love her very much don't you?"

"I suppose I do. She's my mother."

"Say if you suddenly had to do without her?"

There could be no life without her but why was she bewildering me so? Like a blow I remembered my mother had tried to say the same but had healed me with her promise to stay.

"What's the use of supposing? It won't happen," I laughed. "She'll get better. That'll be all."

"Say if she *Died*?"

"She can't die," I shouted, she'd given me such a fright.

"If it happened she did die what would you do?"

"She can't die," I shouted. "She's too young to die. Only old people like Granny die."

We'd been taken by car into the mountains to see my grandmother a last time before she died, the delicate blueberries under the whitethorns on the banks of the lane too narrow for the car. "Just hold on a minute," our uncle said in the cool of the kitchen, halfdoor shut against the hens, and reached up to take a red wad of tenshilling notes from under a teabox on the mantel, "She wants to give these to the children." "Why did you let her do that?" our mother had protested. "Shush. Nothing would do her but for me to change her last few pensions into tenshilling notes to give to the children."

She sat up among pillows in the old bed in the room. Uncle kept his hand against her back as she leaned to kiss us and hand us the red notes. She was grey except for the red about the eyes and she was all bones and the thin red notes shook violently in the bones of her fingers.

A week later all was changed.

The kitchen was full, darkgreen bottles of stout in the window, whiskey, biscuits, fruitcake, plates of cigarettes, rows of clay pipes, lazy swirls of smoke, low hubbub of speech in her praise. She had lived a good and full life though, and like for the rest of us, it had not been all strewn with roses, they were saying. The intense whispering lulled as we were ushered through to the deathroom and rose again as we passed out. From one room to another, two worlds, in the flickering candlelight all changed from the week before, hovering shades of women about the bed. She lay so utterly still between the candles, the eyes were closed, the chin seemed raised, the white hair swept back from the snow pallor of the forehead on which the candles shone in a depth of marble; the black beads she used carry in her apron pocket were twisted through the fingers joined on her breast in prayer, brown Franciscan habit. The stillness was so fierce that it brought terror of fascination to the raised feet beneath the sheet, to touch them to see if they would stir or rock. All I was able to breath was, "Jesus and Mary and Joseph and the child Jesus," over and over in terror of wonder if this picture of utter stillness was the grandmother I used see speak and move. The women signalled us to kneel and pray but we were so frozen they'd to touch us before we obeyed. They'd to touch us again to bless ourselves and rise and leave into the blinding shock of whispering and drinking and smoking and moving in the next room, they were not frozen between candles; drag to go back to the deathroom to see if it had not been all a white dream. My mother could not lie in the terror of that dream of stillness with brown hair.

"My mother has brown hair. She is too young to die. Your hair has to be white before you die."

Bridget Kiernan looked at me and said nothing.

"Isn't she too young to die, Bridget?"

"Yes, my love," she turned away, and unease seeped into the bright sunlight on rails narrowing into the eyes of the distant bridges as I stretched across the white stones between the sleepers home.

Two worlds: the world of the schoolroom in this day, the world of memory becoming imagination; but this last day in the classroom will one day be nothing but a memory before its total obliteration, the completed circle.

In the schoolroom I see the questioning eyes of the children on their teacher.

"You, Johnny," I say to a blond child in the first desk, "Give out the copybooks, and everybody else get out their pens."

I write with a white stick of chalk on the blackboard. Their hands go up as I finish.

"Well, what have I written, Luke?"

"The child is father of the man, sir," he singsongs and a ripple of laughter runs through the class but I do not ask them why today.

"Copy out a page of that in your best handwriting. The writing has been going to the dogs lately. A penny for the best page."

"Can I go to the lavatory first, sir?"

"Go, but tie your shoes or you'll trip."

He smiles up at me as he bends between the desks to tie his laces with small grubby hands and when he's finished I wink back and he laughs as he runs to the door, trying to hold his head and shoulders back manly and straight.

The casual accidents that bring us forth become the certain accident of our going, for if she had not lingered in her classroom that spring evening I would not be: the egg his seed gave my life to should have dropped in its own blood, and I would have remained in Nothingness, as perfectly complete as God on the opposite Pole, a calming thought.

She had tidied the classroom: the scattered pens and pencils, the forgotten mitten; changed the water in the vase that held the narcissi and blue irises before the statue of the Virgin; wiped the day's work from the blackboard except the week's poem she had written up in the corner in red chalk. She then sat to correct the pile of blue exercise books on the desk, savouring a silence that was the more silence because of the absence of the noisy eager bustling that all day had filled the room. She grew so absorbed in the silence and the childish sentences that Mother Mary Martin was in the doorway before she looked up.

"I'm sorry, Kate. Am I interrupting you?"

"Not at all. Please come in, Mother. The few that's left can be finished anytime."

"You've stayed rather late, haven't you?"

"It's more peaceful here than back in the shop and anyhow May'd be expecting me to help her behind the counter."

She'd given her savings to her younger sister to open a sweet and tobacco and stationery shop across from the railway station. They lived in the kitchen at the back, a small curtained judas window on the shop, and in the rooms above it a brother, Michael, who could not read nor write except to scrawl a signature. He had joined them a few months before, and was laboriously learning to drive, in the hope of plying a small hackney car at the station.

"You are still here, Kate. And yet when the bell rings at three most of the lay teachers manage to convey the unfortunate impression that they are leaving a burning building," Mother Mary Martin smiled, her face as pale as the starched white headband that crossed her forehead under the black veil. The long black beads hung still from her girdle. Her eyes fell on the poem in red chalk on the blackboard and she started to read it in a quiet voice, but without any feeling for the rhythm,

HEAVEN-HAVEN

A nun takes the veil

I HAVE desired to go
Where springs not fail,
To fields where flies no sharp and sided hail
And a few lilies blow.

And I have asked to be
Where no storms come,
Where the green swell is in the havens dumb,
And out of the swing of the sea.

"Hopkins," she said and did not go on to the second verse. "I've often noticed those poems in red chalk on the blackboard and meant to ask you about them out of curiosity."

"There's nothing much to tell. Each Monday I write up some short poem, something I like and within the children's reach. We read it together first. Sometimes I point out the word pictures. And then at odd moments, often between classes, we all chant it, until by the week the whole class down to the slowest has it by heart."

"You think it's a good idea?" the Mother's eyes behind the rimless spectacles were smiling.

"What gives me most pleasure still from my own schooling are the poems I learned by heart then; constantly I find them passing through my mind, not unlike old friends or stray strands of music, while I hardly remember anything else with pleasure from the same schooling."

"You may be one in a hundred though. Could it not turn, this learning by rote, the other ninety-nine percent away from poetry? Do you think it infringes the educational rule that we must always proceed to the unknown by way of the known? Do not take this as any criticism. I am only probing."

She paused, wondering whether to avoid the direction the conversation was taking or to let it go on. For years now she'd kept her love of poetry a secret, as defence against the laughter and ridicule it provoked; for years in this small town it had been a secret society of one. She flinched at the memory of Kathleen McCarthy; they'd been playing tennis for hours on the court at the back of the great house at Willowfield, and as they sat, the ball and rackets between them on the lawn, in the wonderful warm glow of the body after fierce excercise, she started quietly to recite *Though you are in your shining days,* and still shivered as she remembered the derision in

Kathleen's laughter when she finished, the singsong that was a vicious mimicry of the poem, "Ah yes, Kate McLaughlin showing off again that she got the gold medal for English in the Carysfort Finals," and her shock into silence for years. She'd learned too that most teachers read little, had even an instinctive hatred of the essential mystery and magic in all real poetry, reducing it to the factual or sentimental and preferably both, four ducks on a pond and a grassbank beyond.

"Doesn't poetry remain always in some way the unknown, Mother?" she ventured after thought. "It can be felt, but not known, as we can never know our own life or another's in the great mystery of life itself."

"I'm afraid, Kate, I don't quite follow."

"Take two descriptions of some simple thing, a day of wind and rain, say. One simply can state it rains and it blows, and yet another description, *The wet winds blow out of the clinging air,* by some magical twist, which I believe is the infusion of the poetical personality into the words, becomes poetry."

"I'm afraid that's above my head, Kate, and it seems to have got far from the question of teaching the children poetry by memorization."

"No, Mother. If the children don't know poems, examples of poetry if you like, how can they ever come to recognize the poetry all about them? Surely the very use of rhyme is secretly to relate lines with one another and make them easy to remember? Or do you think that what I say doesn't make much sense?" She was uneasy, having spoken so freely.

"No. I find what you say interesting but it is outside of me. My bent has always been for the practical."

"And yet you became a nun, Mother?"

"That I did for a practical reason too. It made some sense of my life, gave it, if I might say, a practical purpose. Springs fail in the convent too and more than a few lilies blow, laundry and heating bills and ordinary bickering and bad temper. You've been with us long now, Kate?"

She'd to think back, "It's almost ten years, Mother."

"Often when I think of you it seems you're one of us except you do not wear our habit and live outside the convent. Do you remember how we spoke of you joining us before?"

"Yes, but I am engaged, Mother," she grew self-conscious of the three small rhinestones in the gold on her finger, his ring she'd worn now for six years.

"To put it mildly, hasn't the same engagement dragged on for rather long, as if one or both of you had serious hesitations?"

"Yes, but I've given my promise, Mother."

"Promises are not binding as vows are, especially after such an eccentric engagement, when it is obvious there must be serious doubts and hesitations. Perhaps you'll think it over and we can talk about it again in a week or so?"

"I'll think about it but I cannot promise anything, Mother."

"I don't want you to promise anything, only to think it over," it was the natural time to break off. She put the blue pile of copybooks in the drawer, put on her coat, took up her gloves and handbag. Mother Mary Martin came with her as far as the school steps.

Pale daffodils and narcissi leaned for her from the white iron railing as her crêpesoles went on the gravel of the avenue towards the black cross in its iron circle above the gates. *I will go where springs not fail, where springs not fail, and I have desired to be, out of the swing of the sea,* the phrases sang again and again in her mind. They'd been a thread through her life, many times she had come near acting on them, but what had proved stronger was her passivity, to drift on and let life happen to her rather than to force it into any shape. He'd come a young sergeant into the town, redgold hair and those flashing steel eyes, and swept her off her feet; soon after the engagement he was transferred from the town and she was as happy to let it drift than to ask him for a day; sexual and attractive to women he was able to indulge in a riot of affairs elsewhere, secure in the knowledge that at anytime he could close the book of his summer, and start the respectable autumn of his life with her who waited for him and whom he pedestalled with his mother above these other women. She could still see him standing in the arches of the barracks or leaning over the stone bridge to gaze into the shallow waters that flowed past its walls but now she felt carried high as she walked up Main Street: she would make a bad wife for him, he would find a better, Mother Mary Martin was right, there must be serious hesitations if it had dragged on so long, and only for her constant postponing of things she would have entered the year before she'd met him; she had intended to.

She called out, "God bless the work, James," to James Quinn the butcher, who in his bloodstained apron was scattering fresh sawdust on the floor of his shop out of an old biscuit tin; she called it out with such spirit that it brought him to the door to look who'd spoken before he continued his lazy scattering of the sawdust. Past the grey courthouse, iron chains on its outer wall, to the shop beside the railway, its three stunted firs and one engine blowing steam in the distant sheds. She did not go through the shop, but with her key let herself in by the halldoor so as not to have to speak to her sister, and quietly climbed to her room, strips of bicycle tyre over the lino on the edges of the steps. In a calm fever she wrote him: she was fond of him; she was grateful for the honour he had shown her; he'd soon find someone more practical who'd care for him better than ever she'd be able; for she was called after long thought to enter the convent and dedicate what was left of her life to the service of God in a chain of ordered days. She took the ring from her finger and placed it with the letter in a small cardboard box and took it to the post office where she had it registered. After the fever of the last hours she felt tired as she left the post office. She flinched from the shock and anger she imagined spreading over the face in the Monaghan station when he opened the small box, the redgold hair she'd never comb fingers through, and she did not want to be alone.

As she often did in the evenings after school she decided to walk out the mile of dustroad to her cousin's in Willowfield, trying not to think as she walked, her mind on each plodding step in the dust.

Only the mother and Margaret were in the big farmhouse, and after tea Margaret, a beautiful but unstable girl, took her to listen to some new piano pieces she was practising. As she played Margaret's growing nervousness seemed to pass into her playing, and she could only keep herself from becoming infected by the nervousness by fixing her mind on the vase of honesty reflected in the big mirror but it was with relief she heard the healthy shouts of the two younger sisters come from the links in a rattle of golf clubs. The first thing they noticed was the pale line of skin where the ring had been and asked, "Why are you not wearing your ring, Kate?"

"O, I must have forgot it on the dressing-table," she lied and was disturbed more than she'd thought and wanted to escape from Willowfield, which she did as soon as it was polite, but in the room that overlooked the railway above the shop she could not read and at night found only brief and restless snatches of sleep.

"This is for you, sergeant," the old policeman handed him the packet out of a pile of brown envelopes with the official black harp in the Monaghan station. Carelessly he started to tear it open but when he saw the ring he slipped it into his pocket and left the dayroom. He read the letter in the hallway. Fright changed slowly to anger. He went back into the dayroom.

"I hope you got no bad news, sergeant?" the old policeman's curiosity was up.

"No, but I have to take the day off on a spot of business. Put it in the book. You'll manage for the day without me."

"No bother, sergeant, no bother. It's always useful, a few days' leave in reserve, for you never know what sudden emergency or business may come up," the policeman made a last play for information but he got none.

The sergeant got a white shirt from the woman who came in to do his washing and cleaning and changed out of his uniform into a brown suit. He backed the small Citroën out of the barrack shed and within three hours was knocking on her classroom door. She was at once afraid when she opened the door.

"I got this this morning," he held out the box. "What is the meaning of this?"

"We can't talk here," she said.

"A fine way to get a vocation by breaking an engagement."

"Not here. School will be over in an hour. I'll meet you in the hotel after school."

"Take this then," he handed her the ring in its box. "I don't want it and I'll wait for you in the hotel."

"The bride came down the aisle to the tune of Here Comes the Bride, dressed all in white, looking the picture of death," was found in faded ink among the letters in a trunk after her mother-in-law's death, a description of her wedding day.

"Has it happened to me?" was all her mind could frame over the tea and toast and brown bread of the North Star Hotel breakfast the next morning, the mind already trying to change the sheets and blood and sexual suck of the night into a sacrificial marble on which a cross stood in the centre of tulips and white candles.

"Are you all right?" my father asked between concern and exasperation.

"I'm very happy," she smiled her usual smile.

"Is there anything in particular you'd like to do today?"

"No. Whatever you think would be nice to do."

"The sun is out. I thought we might take a bus out to Sutton Cross and go up to the summit on the top of the tram. If we feel like it we can walk the Cliff path down into Howth for lunch. Sometimes on Sundays we used to do it when I was at the depot."

"I'll get my coat then. It may be cold on the top of the tram."

"Are you sure it's what you'd like to do?"

"I'd love to do it."

The tram and the tramtracks and wires had all gone when we climbed the same path to the summit to go down the cliff walk to look for a room in Howth our first Sunday in Ireland in a holiday of our love. It was the same path that they had ridden on before we were born. Out of dead years they seemed to lean above our lives in fashions that had ceased. Her long thighs stretched against the blue jeans as she climbed, laughing in the pure pleasure of her body and the day in that direct American way I had grown to love. The sea glittered pewter and blue below us. Last of the furze bloom was a ragged yellow on the thorns. Earth and crushed grass were mixed with the smell of the sea.

"How do you know they took this path the day after they were married?"

"She told me."

"What else did they do?"

"They must have gone to Lafayette's, you know the old brown photo, he with the double gold watchchain across his waistcoat, she with the long white dress that drooped away from the throat. They walked streets. Probably were afraid of one another as they always were."

"How soft on the face that wind is from the sea," she said as she was walking.

"And your father and mother?"

"Didn't I tell you? They saw themselves as the beautiful people. I think after the wedding breakfast they drove west towards the deserts. It's funny to think of the man and woman in that yellowed photo riding on that tram up this same path before we were born, the rails gone now, and we walking in their path."

The wind moved in her hair as she strode, glow of the walking in her face. Below us the lighthouse on the sea rocks, a freighter chugging out past the Pigeon House into the bay and nearer small boats tacked with the shadows of their sails.

"And when their honeymoon was over?" she asked.

"He went back to his barracks, she to the convent. They spent holidays with one another. We'll sound like old records soon."

"It wasn't much of a marriage," she mused. "But then look at my two starclimbers."

"That's right from what I saw of the male star. But everything seems to work itself stupidly out. She became pregnant. His mother, my grandmother, moved in to dominate the house. I was born. I would fulfil her dream. One day I would place hands on the chalice while she watched. One day I would say Mass for her soul."

"What do you think of it now?"

"It was the weather of my early life. If it wasn't that weather it would be some other. You had some peculiar early weather too?"

"That's for sure," she laughed, and quickened her stride. "The wind's marvellous on the face."

We walked singly on the beaten cliff path between heather until we came to the sewage outflow. White puffs of the gulls rode delicately far below us on the brown stain in the pewter and blue light of water. A workman, awkward in his Sunday blue, with his wife and three boys had stopped too to look down on the cluster of gulls above the outflow.

"Think of it all piling up out there under the gulls," he was remarking in wonderment.

"Come on. I'm getting hungry," she said.

"We can have stout and brown bread and prawns in the Tavern."

"Then we'll look for the room. I'd love to live out here by the sea."

We started to run when we got to the road, below us the line of the fishing fleet tied up against the far wall of the harbour for the Sunday. We were hungry and thirsty and breathless by the time we reached the Tavern. It was cool and dark within after the sealight and we were the first customers.

"Here's to it all piling up out there under the gulls," as we raised our glasses of black with their collar of cream.

A large black fly comes through the window of the classroom of this last day, and hubbub starts. It careers wildly round before clinging high to the far wall.

"Can I, sir?" the blond boy in the first desk raises his book.

"No," I refuse but know there will be no quiet till the fly is killed or driven out. The excitement bubbles higher as I take the newspaper from the table and climb on a desk. A shout goes up as the fly falls with the first blow of the rolled newspaper. The boy below me picks it from the floor by a wing and holds it high like a trophy.

"There must be quiet," I shout at them to be still. The boy lets go of the dead fly's wing. The others look curiously at me for a moment and the dead silence becomes a murmur as they return to their books. I think out of what couplings they must have come. They have all certificates of birth and will all one day have death certificates but their certificates of conception would be more interesting.

"It was those two bottles of the Special Offer white wine from Powers that did it," after rare sirloin and kicking the hot water bottle out on the floor. In a lane off Parnell Square hot from dancing in the National. In the thick juice of passion or in dry compliance, but I tire of the cruelty of the play, and turn back to my own life.

My mother's dream for my life, the way that life happened down to the schoolroom of this day, my memory of it and the memory of her dream, and so the tide is full, and turns out to her life; and what a coffin this schoolroom would be without the long withdrawing tide of memory becoming imagination.

My dead parents were probably glad to leave the North Star Hotel at the end of the week's honeymoon, I find myself telling my love; and almost at once he'd to return to his barracks, and the next Monday she went back to the convent school. For a short time nothing was changed, except he came the two days he had free from the barracks each month and slept with her in the room above the shop, and she went to spend odd weekends in the big empty livingquarters of the barracks; but this did not last long, for there grew a natural antipathy between him and her sister that was to increase to hatred with the years, and after a quarrel over a razor blade he'd left on the sink they rented a bungalow for her on the edge of the town. Two could live cheaper than one, he reasoned, now he had the expense of three homes, and he told his mother, the tall proud dressmaker who had come in severe black to their wedding and who'd written that the bride came down the aisle looking the picture of death, to close the cottage by the sea where she had brought him up, and move to the bungalow. She came with her trunks and sewing gear to the bungalow without the slightest show of emotion and immediately took over the running of the house down to the minutest detail.

Yet nothing even then was much changed. He slept his two free nights with her each month in the bungalow instead of above the shop and now when she went the odd weekends to the barracks the old woman came with her. She was always glad when her mother-in-law decided to remain some days behind in the barracks with her son, for what she found hardest about the bungalow was the difficulty of not being alone. Even when she was in her room reading the old woman would follow her there with a glass of hot milk or some other excuse, "You can break your health with too much reading." "I have to read for my work," she would lie. "I don't know. In my day teachers didn't need to read much once they'd got their papers," but what she pursued her most with was why wasn't she pregnant, she was a young woman yet. When this was given another twist by her husband, "You know I don't mind, Kate, but people are wondering about why you're not expecting yet," she felt quite hunted and it was with relief she discovered herself pregnant at the end of the second long school holiday in the barracks. They'd be satisfied now, and she'd to smile that as soon as the pregnancy was confirmed the old woman started to sew for the child. As she saw the skilful hands of the old dressmaker turn out the small clothes she felt uneasy. "Aren't we jumping too far ahead?" she tried to protest but it ended with the old woman admonishing her not to lift anything heavy, to drink milk, a bottle of Guinness a day would be good.

"Often I think it's she that's having the child and not me," she confessed wryly to her sister in the shop and now that she didn't want to read and to avoid the bungalow and the old woman's sewing and fussing over her she spent long hours in the church after school. "If it is a boy it will one day raise the chalice in anointed hands and if a girl it will live in the ordered days of the convent and not in this confusion of a life," she prayed.

She noticed how he hardly ever stayed any nights now that she was pregnant, finding excuse to return to the barracks; but when the child was born, used to the attention of the two women and finding himself supplanted, he was furious.

"The child is being ruined. Every time he opens his mouth one or the other of you run to him."

"Then you were ruined," his mother told him sharply.

"A child should be fed at regular times not every time he cries."

"A child only cries when it needs attention."

"Well, if you want to ruin the child at least I have the authority to see that you're not let."

He got milk, bottles, a little copper burner, a saucepan and clock and locked himself in the room with the child that was once me. He was nothing if not demonstrative, "The child will have to learn regular feeding times, not be ruined with spoiling every time it cries."

The mother fretted downstairs. The violence paralysed her. It was the grandmother and the father who struggled. The child seemed less and less her child.

"Do you want the child to choke?" it was the old woman she heard beat on the locked door. "The child will be fed in four hours time and no sooner," she heard him shout back.

When the crying grew hysterical he lifted it from the cot, it stilled for a moment, but sensing the unfamiliar hands broke out even more hysterically. He felt like smashing it against the wall. Long before the four hours were up he abandoned it.

"The child is ruined past correction. You've ruined him and let the old woman ruin him," he scolded her before leaving for the barracks while the grandmother comforted the child in the bedroom.

4

Already the feeling was deep within her that there was nothing, nothing on earth, she could do; and that small failure of domination she saw him revenge two years later, "With those curls you'll have the child growing up imagining it's a girl," and both the women wept as they watched the gold curls fall from the shears on to the newspaper under the chair on the cement. I have to smile wryly as I think that I was that child or pawn. Was my life beaten into its shape in this schoolroom day by those forces or would it have grown similar even if the forces were otherwise . . . ?

I remember the sun, the flaming ball of heaven, always seemed reachable when it rested on the hawthorns high on the hill towards evening; and I climbed away from the bungalow, stumbling in the hooftracks and against the clumps of rushes that seemed tall then, and crawled on all fours through the whitethorns. My heart pounded with the excitement of being about to take the sun in my hands. When I pushed through the whitethorns and climbed out of the briars of the dry drain the other side there was the sun, calm and burning miles away on the next hill, cattle grazing and two hares playing in the rushes of the valley between, and with the tiredness and disappointment I fell asleep and slept till close to dark, when I was woken by many voices anxiously calling my name about the hill.

The old woman railed at me for the anxiety I had caused when they took me down the hill. She found me another time throwing newspaper on the fire in the child's fascination of flame, "Lessons will have to be taught," and took and put my finger in the fire and as I screamed she quietly held me on her knee to smear ointment on the burn saying, "Now you know what fire is, love."

I had started to go to school with my mother, and my grandmother's dominion began to be eroded until I went down with whooping cough. She at once moved me into her room, barring access to everybody; and when my mother pleaded that at least the doctor should be called in she refused, and sent instead into the mountains for a stallion. I remember being carried out in a pile of blankets, the sky darkblue and the night bright with the stars of a night of frost, a man holding the stallion by the bridle ring, and the stars in the clear sky as I was passed three times under the stallion in the name of the Father and Son and Holy Ghost, and my mother's tense face in the starlight as she said, "I think we should send for the doctor now as well," my grandmother calmly handing the man silver coins with ringing of iron as the stallion stamped in the cold.

The proud old woman fell ill as soon as I was better and fiercely protesting was taken to the hospital. One Sunday I was dressed in blue with white ankle socks to visit her there. My mother and father both paused at the ward door and my mother said, "She'd like it better if he gave her the grapes," and I was handed the grapes in their brown paperbag. There were nine or ten other old women in the ward and she was more bones than flesh in the iron bed. Some of the black grapes crushed when they lifted me to her lips. She stroked my hair and immediately started to complain to my father and mother but I didn't follow what she was complaining of. As we left she wanted to make me a present of the grapes but my father wouldn't allow it. I never saw her again. When I'd ask about her I'd get some vague answer.

New sisters started arriving each year. The bungalow grew too small. They bought a twostoried farmhouse closer to the school and moved there. My father came much oftener to the farm, draining and cutting hedges; and I started to move deeper into the shelter of my mother, away from the cold shadow my father cast.

I remember him trying to win me away. He bought me a bicycle. I was to use the bicycle to go to him at Easter. I cycled to the station. The bicycle went in the guard's van and the fireman who lodged with my aunt put me off at Drumshambo. My father met me halfway between the railway station and the barracks and we cycled back together.

The great empty rooms of the barracks rang with echoes, and I felt the tedium all children feel waiting on adults, my life suspended till he was free; and in order to charm me he made the adult's mistake of coming down to what he imagined was the child's level. Instead of charming me he became rather frightening and unreliable, a caricature of what I knew. The evening before I was to leave he took me on the Oakport walk, the great avenue on which carriages had driven round the lake to Oakport House, the grey cutstone of the walls intact but the gates with the coat of arms in wrought iron fallen, the sun above the firs across the lake bright on the ironroof of the boathouse and the beechwoods deep in the fields.

"Wouldn't you like to come and live with me here?" he suddenly asked.

"I have to live with the others in Aughoo."

"You could live with me instead in the barracks. We'd have great times together."

"But I have to go to school in Aughoo."

"You could go to school here just as well. To Mrs. Mullaney."

I was silent for I was lost for another excuse and I was afraid.

"Wouldn't you have a much better time here living in the barracks than in a house full of women? I'd take you shooting and fishing. For instance, could you say *shit* or *piss* before women?"

"No."

"You'd have to say *weewee* or *job*, isn't that right?"

"That's right."

"With a man you could say those words. Those things don't shock a man. With a man you can be much more free when there are no women around."

"But I'd have to tell them in confession anyhow," I said gravely in a frightened voice.

He went suddenly still. He made an impatient gesture with his hand and quickened his walk as if he knew he'd blundered. We walked past the Roman arches of the brokendown coach-house to where the firs began and turned without entering the woods. The failing light lay even more gently on the water and on the broken reedstems along the shore where the black puffs of waterhens moved.

"You wouldn't think of staying even a few days extra? A few days off from school'd be neither here nor there."

"They'd be worried if I didn't go back tomorrow. Jim Brady will be looking out for me at the station. He said he'd let me ride back in the engine."

"All right. I won't stand in your way so but don't tell anybody when you get back what we've been talking about. They might read into it wrong."

I nodded in vigorous agreement. I was only too glad not to have to talk or think about it more, as a flight of widgeon that had been disturbed upriver curved well away from us as they came down into the bay.

He started to come constantly to the farm after that, as if he was finding the barracks empty and lonely for the first time; and in spring he persuaded her to offer her resignation and for us all to move to the barracks and begin life there as a normal family. She cycled to the presbytery to offer her resignation but the priest refused pointblank to accept it. She'd lose her independence, he said; and dropped dark hints that her husband was not a normal person and that it wouldn't work.

He was furious when he heard, but he was not prepared to confront the priest's authority with his own, and the plan was let rest: but he continued to come as often from the barracks and he began to be exasperated by the running of the farm and especially by what he thought of as her whimsical waste of money.

Always he looked for flaws. The house was so full of his fury the evening he found catshit in the loose oats he'd stored in the backroom, the yellow grains encrusted on the dried pieces of shit, that I went and climbed into the cover of the big ash from which we used to swing. I must have sat hours there, torn between the boredom of the tree and desire to remain out of sight till he'd gone. I saw him out on the cinders with relief, for he had his coat and bicycle clips on. He was much calmer than after his discovery of the catshit in the oats, but he was still nagging my mother, who had her arms crossed and she was following her brown shoes as they moved on the cinders, but instead of him taking his bike from the wall as I'd hoped they turned towards me in the tree. I watched the board of the swing that hung on a rope from the branch where I sat as they drew close.

"The cats in the oats are bad enough but going through those figures shows there's neither care nor head nor tail on this house." He'd given her a large police ledger earlier in which she was supposed to enter all expenses. She hated having to deal with the figures.

"You know I'm useless with figures," she said quietly.

"You can add and subtract, can't you? Otherwise it'll be the poorhouse. And soon we'll have the children's education to think about."

"Others get by somehow," she said tentatively.

"What has others got to do with us?" he mouthed in exasperation.

"It's not easy to save. There seems always something or other."

"Those damned sponging relatives of yours, I suppose!"

"No. That's not fair," she took two brown notes from her pocket. "That's all that's left this quarter but if you imagine that you must have them. I was in fact going to buy sandals."

"A start has to be made somewhere," he quietened as he smoothed out the notes. "They can go barefoot. It's healthier. The trouble with you is that you're too soft and you've never known what real want is. The old woman that's gone and I knew what want is," and he began the story of the shopping bag, told so obsessively often over the years that we grew to know it as our own story, though in each telling old details were often dropped in favour of new.

This day in the schoolroom I try to trace it out a last time, some of the detail inaccurate too, but the story still the same. His father had come back to the island from New York, a returned barowner, and bought the small cottage by the shore.

As soon as he settled in the cottage he looked round the island for a wife and found the young girl who was to become my hard proud grandmother. She was apprenticed to the island dressmaker then. After a year my father was born and they lived quietly, and in the eyes of the islanders prosperously, till the child was three. The old man suddenly received a letter from America, saying there was trouble with the partner he'd left in charge of the bar, and that he'd to return to New York at once. He'd send money and come back as soon as he'd straightened out the affairs of the bar, he told her. For some years small sums came regularly but there was no mention of the bar or any immediate possibility of his return and then suddenly the small sums stopped. She used what she'd saved at first, and the island shop gave them credit, and there began what he called the "horrible watching of the postman", as he walked with my mother below me close to where the board moved on its rope.

"Has Patrick come into sight yet?" she'd ask, I heard him tell.

"No. Not yet, mother."

"It's a bit early yet," she'd look slowly up at the crawl of the clock.

"He's at Reilly's now," I'd come in from the road, rocks sloping away from its hoof- and tyre-marked dirt down to the sea.

"They'll probably have him in for a cup of tea."

"No. He's coming this way. He had nothing for them. Will I go to the gate to wait for him?"

"No. He'd know we were waiting."

Far back in the room we'd watch through the lace curtain that filtered the sea, holding our breath when he came near a big stone in the wall where he'd start to dismount if he had a letter or parcel, following him past the gate and beyond in the hope he'd forgotten the letter, and when I'd look at her she'd say, "No. It must be delayed till tomorrow," and turn away to lose herself in dusting or some small task.

Credit grew tighter in the shop; Paddy Joe in his blue

overalls behind the counter, trammel nets and bright gallons and rope and bicycle tyres hanging from the ceiling, behind the wooden partition the low buzz of the fishermen drinking in the bar, started to grumble, "I'll do it this time but credit is getting terrible tight," as he halved the pound of butter with a greasy bacon knife.

"The money is due any day from America. It's the first time in years it's been late," she'd to swallow her pride.

"Well, some of those monies better come soon from America because that's what they're all telling me and it's no use to me when I have to face into the bank manager," he said as he added up her bill and struck it on top of others on a large nail above the till.

When waiting for the postman to come grew too painful she took to crossing the hill to the spring when he was about to come and when she saw from the hill that he was safely past she had to refrain herself from dashing down to the door but each day she opened the door the cement inside was as empty of any letter as ever before.

"I should have thought of it sooner," she said a Saturday he had cranked past into the wind without stopping. "You know what has happened. He has sent us more money than usual and he was afraid they'd bungle it in the local post office. What he's done is registered it and sent it to the main office in Derry, meaning for us to go in and collect it. We have still time to get the eleven bus."

We dressed, and she took the big oilcloth shopping bag, made up of black squares and red. She was excited on the bus. When they'd collected the registered letter she counted out how she'd fill the shopping bag: raisins, oranges, prunes, lemons, rice, smoked ham, caraway. She was like a girl again.

Once she left the bus she grew hard and I remember walking towards the post office in the shelter of that hardness as I have seen foals move in the mare's shadow and stood by her elbow at the counter as she gave the name and address to the clerk and asked if a registered letter had come for her from America.

He wrote down the name and disappeared behind a partition of wood and cathedral glass. We heard the slow leafing through a bundle of envelopes. His hands were empty when he came out.

"Nothing," he shook his head.

"Would you just give one more look? I'm certain it must have come," she said.

He repeated the name blankly and went again behind the partition. He came back with a bundle of letters, "This is the lot."

He leaned sideways inside the counter as he went through the bundle a second time so that they both could read. There was nothing.

"There's no others?" she was white as she asked.

"I'm sorry but that's the lot."

"It must be late so," she lifted the shopping bag of red and black squares, "But thanks."

We stood when we got to the street.

"What'll we do now, mother?"

"Wait for the bus, my love."

"Will the letter ever come now?"

"I don't know. Maybe it won't come now."

We hung idle about the town, drifting between the windows, and finally went to the shelter to wait for the bus. I remember the metal clasp of the purse as she fumbled for the few coins of the fare. When the bus got to the causeway to the island, rocking from pothole to pothole, she told me to tell the driver to stop; but before I had time to leave the seat she was violently sick, lifting the empty shopping bag to her mouth. She told the driver not to wait and we stood on the road and watched the bus go, passengers staring back at us through the dusty windows. When the bus had gone we left the road and sat on the rocks a few feet above the sea.

"I'll be all right in a little while," she said and when some colour started to come back to her cheeks she turned the shopping bag inside out and went down to the water and washed the vomit from the oilcloth in the sea.

For the rest of that year we lived on what she could get from dressmaking and on the mussels where the fresh water ran from the lake in rivulets between the black rocks at the low tide and nettles she clipped with her scissors into the spring-water can.

"When I grow up we'll never be poor, mother," I said to her, and though she is gone I'm not going to be poor now either, and "we'll have to make a serious effort to save," he said to my mother smoothing out the two fivers as they went back to his bicycle that leaned against the wall of the house.

I was able to breath freely and to start to come down from the branch as they walked slowly with the bicycle up the cinder path to the road.

Summer and winter he came then from the barracks on that bike and each year a new child arrived in the house.

I think of him the winter night he came with the black whippet.

He'd have locked the living quarters of the barracks, put on his pullups and cape, lit the blue flame of the carbide lamp, and come down to Mullins in the dayroom to sign himself out on two days' leave.

Old Mullins would rise himself out of his comfortable doze before the fire, listen to the rain beat on the slates, and rise as soon as he heard the heavy boots on the cement and fix himself into an uncomfortable stance by the mantel. Nothing was served or unserved by this awkward stance, but Mullins felt discomfort had the wondrous appearance of virtue, and that the sergeant would be less likely to snipe at him in this position than if he found him comfortably slumped in the chair. The black whippet followed him into the dayroom.

"You've a bad night for travelling, sergeant."

"It's not good," he said as he signed in the thick ledger.

"And you're taking the whippet, I see."

"He's no use here."

Mullins wasn't comfortable until he had left. He waited till he heard tyres on the gravel, the carbide lamp and dark shape waver past the streaming window, and lifted the newspaper for another time that day. A Georgian house in Killiney with four bedrooms, a large garden and views of the sea was for sale, he read: in another hour he'd take the phone off the hook and chance it to the pub for a few good jorums that'd carry him through the night.

In the same night my father pushed behind the tunnel the hissing carbide lamp made in the rain, the patter of the whippet's gallop behind the swish of wheels, trees moving round the lighted hearts of houses along the way. As he started to sweat under the cape he thought of trees he could sell on the farm to push farther out of mind the mouth of the shopping bag in that bus, or did he dream he was young? He was in a railway carriage. It was lighted and the five other people were reading magazines. Photos of castles and rivers hung on the walls. *All Change* was shouted out. A red lantern swung. The stone of the station was harsh and empty under the naked bulbs as the loose wheels of a few trollies rattled. He was climbing the gangplank on to the waiting ship. He'd have a drink at the bar, engage some stranger in idle conversation, knowing that the girl in dark hair would meet the boat in the morning, and all day they'd lie in each other's arms, the hot tiredness of the journey beating into her opening flesh.

There was suddenly one lighted caravan in the forecourt of the limestone quarry at Keshcarrigan. He was halfway. As he turned round by the quarry into the village he was so hot under the cape and pullups he thought he'd break the journey and rest.

"Is it all right to let the dog in?" he asked the man at the far end of the long counter.

"Sure. It's neither night for man or beast," the little bald old man answered and wiped the counter with a dirty rag.

When he heard rats race on the boards overhead he decided to have whiskey instead of stout. The panting whippet lay down in the sawdust in front of the red halforange of the oilheater in the fireplace, above it a small mantel and a mirror with gilt, and the red hand of Bushmills.

"That's a well fed cat you have," he referred to a black

cat eyeing the whippet from the safety of a barstool as the rats raced overhead.

"Red lazy," the genial answer came and the conversation drifted to cattle and customers and rain. He had a second whiskey and after the undemanding few words and glow of the alcohol he left feeling completely restored. Another hour found him facing the red lantern of the closed railway gates of Ballinamore. As he'd to wait for the coal train to come in before they'd open he decided to call at his sister-in-law's shop, its lighted windows facing the three stunted fir trees inside the railway wall.

"Old shiteyarse," she called him but never in his presence, and he never missed any chance to annoy her. Knowing her obsessive tidiness he went into the shop, nodded to the girl behind the counter, opened the leaf and door and let the wet whippet into her kitchen.

"O my God, that bloody dog," she reacted at once, lifting the dripping whippet by the collar out the back door. "To bring a dirty dog into a clean kitchen on a night like this."

"What a hard woman to put a poor dog out on a night like this," he laughed with pleasure but she was never more dangerous than when in this mood. "And where, may I ask, is the pain located tonight?" she struck at his hypochondria.

"You bloody bitch," he muttered under his breath and turned to go.

"Won't you stay and have a hot cup of tea?" she could rub the salt in now.

"No," he said gruffly. "I just dropped in as the gates were shut."

"You're welcome to a cup."

"No. I have to go. Do you have any messages for them in Aughoo?"

"Tell her I'll come out on Sunday."

With folded arms she followed him out through the shop. The whippet had come round from the back and lay beside the bicycle in the rain.

"Old shiteyarse," she repeated as she watched the bicycle

disappear through the now open railway gates while *Where is the pain located now?—the bloody bitch*, flamed in anger in his mind for the last four miles of the road till he arrived soaked, the whippet's paws bleeding from the stones as it thirstily lapped water, while he changed out of cape and pullups at the foot of the stairs, leaving small pools on the cement, but in two days he was gone again.

Christmas was coming, the last Christmas she'd be well. Cinnamon, nuts, raisins, oranges, lemons, sage, cloves, almonds, currants, crystals, ginger, figs, wine, she gave me one of the lists as we stood on the gravel of the platform for the train to come in, "You musn't let me forget any of these." The second list she put secretly away in her handbag.

Most of the others waiting were women, wives of welltodo farmers ashamed to be seen on their husbands' carts or traps. They'd meet their husbands in town, heap the carts with their Christmas purchases, and return on the train as elegantly empty-handed as they'd set out, the fur and little paws and snouts of foxes about their throats. They all nodded to my mother, and some of the bolder came up to her to enquire about their children's progress. I heard her say *sensitivity* and *late developer* and *good placid child*, words I would hear later in my voice, disguising what the parents did not want to hear about their hopes.

Plumes of smoke above the distant rookery into which the rails ran as one shining thread was the first sign of the train before it came out of the trees—a black engine, two carriages, and a guard's van swaying perilously behind—and chugged up to the station. The station-master's red flag waved it to a stop it seemed only all too anxious to obey. S.L. & N.C.R. was written on the carriages. Sligo Leitrim and Northern Counties Railway but as a woman's voice shouted the old pun Slow Late And Never Come Right there was a polite titter. A green flag was waved when all had scrambled aboard. Wheezing and spluttering it got under way and as it did another woman shouted *Yahoo* and there was less restrained laughter. We sat and watched the slow fields but we did not speak, awkward in the presence of so many people who were neither familiars nor complete stranger. Michael, her brother, was waiting in his hackney car at the town station. He offered to drive us to the shop, but she refused, knowing it was his busiest time of year. We walked the few hundred yards past the three stunted firs to the shop, its windows full of lights and Christmas.

We opened the door into the small well of the shop through which my father had come with the whippet. May was in the shop, serving a man cigarettes; and then she crossed to the other side of the shop to help a woman choose toys, motioning she would be with us in a minute. As soon as she'd sold the woman a doll and a fire engine my mother said, "Why don't you let us go in? I know you're busy."

"No. I'll be in with you. Mary can take care of the shop. The rush won't come till evening. It's only to get away from that so-and-so with the hat I came out and sent Mary in."

"You mean James Sharkey?"

"Who else do you think—complete with hat and hangover. He's been pestering me this hour to know if Kate'll be in on the train for Christmas Eve."

She lifted the leaf and we went through into the kitchen. They knew one another's ways so well—or Mary knew my aunt's—that she at once left off what she was doing and took her place in the shop. James Sharkey rose from his chair at the fire to shake our hands as my aunt said sarcastically, "Well, at least you won't have to pester me whether they're coming in on the train or not anymore."

He smiled and bowed. He was tall, in a wellcut grey suit and he wore a brown hat with a band. His features were strikingly handsome and regular, but the skin was stained with whiskey and heart disease.

"Pestering me all morning to see if you were coming in, and now that they're in I suppose you'll have one more cup of tea?"

"Since you ask so nicely I don't see how I can very well refuse," he answered with gentle sarcasm and she snorted.

Mother laughed, a low silvery laugh, it was an old play between them; for May basically liked Sharkey, disapproving only of his eternal brown hat and drinking, "Does the man sleep in it?"

It was easy to see how handsome he must have been on leaving the Training College, with curly black hair, and there were photos of him with young girls in summer about the Austin Seven or the Baby Austin, as it was called, he drove then. He had his pick of the girls, but had fallen disastrously in love with Kathleen McCarthy and he'd started to haunt Willowfield. She went on golfing and playing tennis and working like a boy with her father in the fields and would not listen to him while he prematurely went bald. He gave up his suit only when he decided he was finally bald and put on those brown hats that no one ever saw him without since and took to drink.

There was some trouble at first when he started to attend Mass with his hat on, but the priest was a practical man—seeing that under no circumstances was he prepared to uncover his head, and that he himself couldn't very well have him in church with his hat on, he had the collection table moved out to the porch and had him collect the coins into the small blue bags there every Sunday ever since. Since the porch wasn't technically in the body of the church he could wear his hat there. As he spoke with my mother of school reports and inspectors his voice had a gentleness and melancholy that seemed not to belong to the subjects.

Jimmy, their oldest brother, came with a branch of berried holly from the mountain farm where they'd grown up together. Michael dropped in for tea between runs, he was on his way into the heart of the country for an old couple; and James Sharkey, feeling excluded by the intimacy of the brothers and sisters, rose and said he'd be on his way.

"I suppose he won't get past Terry's without a large whiskey and chaser," May complained.

"Ah, he's all right," Jimmy chided gently.

"It's all right for you talking when you haven't to look at

the spectacle of him and his hat practically every day."

"He was unlucky," Jimmy said.

"Wasn't there other fish in the sea?"

"Will any of yous be out at the home place over the Christmas?" Jimmy changed and all four felt at once the different things they had left to do with their day.

The shopping was all done, the day almost ended, the lights burning ghostly on the white gravel of the station as we waited loaded with parcels for the train to take us home, steam and sparks coming from the sheds across the tracks. The levelcrossing gates were shut. The row of yellow-steamed windows came slowly in behind the big engine. Some of the women had had drinks and bantered dangerously.

"Watch the van doesn't go off the rails as it did at Kiltubrid," a woman with the little fox loose about her throat shouted at Hughie McKeon, the guard.

"I'll watch," he smiled back about the night he almost lost his life and waved his green flag for the train to go out.

"It's toys you have in that bag?" I pressed my mother about what she'd bought in secret and she smiled but did not answer.

"There's no Santa. There's only toys you bought in town. I am old enough to be told," I held my breath as I searched her face, hoping she'd deny my fear.

"I'm old enough," I pressed as I waited.

"You promise not to spoil it for the others so?" she said quietly.

"Of course I promise."

"You are right but you must not tell."

"So you leave the toys in the room while we sleep?"

"Yes. You're old enough to know but you promised not to tell."

"I'll not tell, mother."

I blushed at the memory of nights trying to stay awake to see or catch the redcoated figure with his sack and then I shuddered. It was the first break in the sea of faith that had encircled me, for what if God was but the same deception. I shuddered as if I felt already that the journey would be dark and inland through sex and death, the sea continually withdrawing. I was glad to turn to my mother who was explaining that the myth of Santa Claus was originally Christian and derived from St. Nicholas. She told me about the life of St. Nicholas and argued that Santa Claus could be said to exist in a truer but more complicated way than childish belief. For as the priest re-enacted daily the Last Supper and His Passion and death in the Mystery of the Mass, in the same way each Chirstmas parents re-enacted the beautiful life of St. Nicholas so that in that way it was still completely true. I was glad to listen to my clever mother and the lazy beat of the train and the tinkle of tipsy laughter, as Hughie McKeon went round collecting the tickets, in order to stay out of my own mind.

It was to be the last natural Christmas.

There were two doctors in the house at Easter, whispered consultations. My father came. She left for a Dublin hospital. We were transferred to the barracks, changing to the school there till she'd come out of hospital. In my anxiety I began to wonder over my grandmother for the first time in years: where had she faded to after I'd taken her the black grapes in hospital ... The evenings alone were peaceful, watching my father's one policeman Mullins on his yellow chair on the gravel outside the dayroom, a hundred white flintstones by his side. He aimed each stone at the top strand of wire above the nettingwire on the garden. If the aim was true, the stone falling in a slow arc, the wire rang through all its steel posts to the iron gate past the lavatory at its end, and Mullins would burst into a laugh of triumph; but mostly they missed and fell safely into the onion bed beyond. When he'd exhausted the pile he'd rise from the chair and we'd both gather the stones out of the onions and the beaten grass below the wire.

"Do you think will she be long in?" I'd sometimes ask as we gathered the stones.

"She'll not be long. Mind you I wouldn't mind a bit of a spell in hospital myself, with nothing serious of course, something minor that gives a man a chance to be waited on and rest," more or less similar versions of the reassuring answer would always come, and we'd trudge back through the gate; he'd sit on the yellow chair, curve the white stones towards the wire, the wire ringing five or eight times out of every slow hundred; and then she came home the day the pheasant was shot for her.

She must have stayed three or four days in the barracks. And then to my joy she asked if I could go alone with her ahead of the others to open the farmhouse. I'd have two whole days, world, alone with her.

My aunt had already opened the house when we got there, a fire was burning, and everything aired and clean. My aunt stayed for some hours talking with her and I never forgot the rich happiness and peace of the house when she left, my beloved was home, and I was alone with my beloved.

She'd said it'd be nice to walk to Priors for milk before sleep. We took the can and went by the railway and up the avenue of old trees that were clear in a moon over the lake. The ring of the aluminium cup mixed with voices saying how glad they were she was back as they took our measure of milk from the churn on the brown flagstones. When we walked home under the trees and saw the moonlit water and grey sand of the road it was as if the whole night was full of healing. "Never, never go away again," I made her promise as she kissed me goodnight, already resenting the intrusion of the others on the morrow.

Loss and the joy of restoration, sweet balm of healing: already that shape must have been on all the faces bent over their books in this the classroom of the day. What a little room it would be without memory of the dead and dead days, each day without memory a baby carriage in the shape of a coffin wheeled from the avenue of morning into night.

I wonder if any of them know it is to be my last day with them in the room but I do not ask. I have no regrets. I see this day as logical. When its shape is completed it will be seen to have grown as naturally in its element as the trees that lean away from the sea.

My mother had a breast removed in the hospital, she was without that breast as we walked in the balm of that evening for the milk and back; and she'd been warned that under no circumstances must she get pregnant. There was a risk that if any of the cancer still remained in the opening of the ductal glands it would pour into the whole bloodstream.

I turn to memory and images out of my own life to imagine the night that she conceived.

Counting back from the birth of the child it must have been the wet night he came from the barracks on the bicycle with the whippet. Small pools lay on the cement about his rainwear at the foot of the stairs. They stayed over the weakening fire till the house was asleep. She lit the candle on the window and climbed ahead of him, the candle in the blue tinholder showing them the way to their room at the end of the corridor.

"Is it all right?" he drew her to him.

"It's a dangerous time."

"I'll be careful," starved for sexuality he could not hold back.

She turned to him: it was her duty.

He meant to be careful, but moving in the warm dark flesh of the woman the male urge to inflict the seed deep within her grew and it was too late when he pulled free. "It'll be all right," he said, but he was uneasy, that pang of pleasure seemed very little now when set against the risk. He listened to her get out of bed to do something a moment in the darkness before coming back between the sheets.

"It'll be all right," he caressed her mechanically but was uneasy and could not sleep in spite of his tiredness.

"I'm sure," she murmured and turned into the quiet fatalism of, "One way or another it will be the will of God," and she slept by his restless side, for he felt if he'd got her pregnant that neither the pleasure nor the darkness would pardon a birth and a death in that one pang, the pang that now was so weak that it had never happened.

Mornings that spring, on our way to school, she'd hand me her bag, and I'd watch a stream of grey vomit pour from her mouth into the nettles of the margin. She wasn't able to return to the school after the summer holidays and employed a substitute. The child was born in late October. A few weeks later she struggled back to the school—by breaking her sick leave she qualified again for full salary for another six months—but as soon as she fulfilled the technicality she employed another substitute and the doctor started to come to the house every second day.

I see especially her brother, my uncle Michael, who'd the hackney car, climb those same stairs as the doctor's satchel so often climbed. Often I was sitting on the sill of the bedroom when he came.

The windows were blinded, so coming from the daylight he'd grope his first step into the room.

"So you're awake," he'd stumble. "And the boy is with you too," he'd see.

"It's good of you to come," she'd hold out her hand and he'd ask me about a white bullock he had on the land that I hand fed for him.

"How's the patient today?"

"Much as usual."

"You'll have to make a start soon. You won't find till summer is on us."

She smiled at his goodnatured awkwardness. Of course the summer always came, I feel she must have thought. And yet even in summers there comes the moment when the flowers are frozen and the swinging tassel of the blind stops dead, the instant of the life as it meets its end.

"Will you be driving Miss Mullins up to her home in Donegal this weekend?"

"I think so," he blushed.

Miss Mullins was her present substitute, all these young substitutes were untrained and were paid two-thirds of the minimum teacher's scale out of her salary. He was ever falling in love with these young women, who were content to dally with him, while they waited for their lives to happen on the meagre pay.

"Tell her I can have her wages sent to school if it's awkward for her to come here."

"I think she said she was coming to see you this Friday."

"That's fine then."

"Do you think you'll be needing her for much longer?" he asked tensely.

"Till at least the summer holidays," she said and he relaxed; he'd have her company for all that time, though it depended on his sister being ill till then.

"We must have you better by then. There's nothing you want me to do in town?" he said, veering towards the door.

"Nothing at all but thank you for coming."

Hope grew about her in any corner it could take root.

Aunt May heard a Nurse O'Neill had lately come home from England. On the halfday, she asked me to cycle with her to O'Neill's. If we could persuade the young nurse, who had got a gold medal in her Finals, to come and nurse mother all would be well.

An old woman in black met us at the door of the three-roomed cottage, asbestos having replaced its thatch, flowering currants straggling against the whitewashed stones of the wall.

"She came home for a rest, you know, not to work after having pneumonia," the old woman said authoritively with folded arms, and our hopes fell.

"Can't I have a word with her anyhow?" my aunt pleaded. The old woman called to an inner room and a strong blond girl I had seen one summer on the camogie field came out. She had in her hand the book she'd been reading. She offered the same objection as her mother. She had come home to rest. My aunt pleaded with her, using a jargon of "us depending on her to come, a mother with children, there was already a maid so that there'd be no household work".

The blonde girl weakened and looked to the mother, who gestured with her shoulders, "It's your decision."

"All right. As long as it's understood I can leave if I find it too much," and our hearts sang. Hours and wages were quickly agreed and we cycled home drunk with joy. All would be well now, we said to one another, and the hedgerows of the lanes we cycled on were again marvellous.

Nurse O'Neill came the next day and a stricter order of meals and bedtime and silence was imposed on the house but nothing else changed. And in a few weeks a night nurse was needed too and the doctor found a Nurse McCaffrey.

My father didn't come to the house anymore. He fell on excuse after excuse and finally cried that it was too painful for him to see her the way she was now. Her family were very angry but nothing would persuade him to come.

Alone between the night nurse and the day I like to imagine she spent much time in the mountains, in that day she remembered with such vividness.

She was home on holidays from the Marist convent where the King's Scholarship kept her a boarder. It had been hot all that summer in the mountains, shapes of hooves had set so rockhard that you stumbled if you tried to run in the fields, and the slabs of butter were wrapped in the big cabbage leaves. Haytime was almost over, her father scything the margins of the meadows, where scutch and briar so quickly blunted the edge that he tired of using the soft sandstone, sent her to the house for the new emery stone he'd put off using all summer, warning her to be careful bringing it back.

"Be careful with it or there'll be murder, after him hoarding it so long," her mother warned her again as she took the delicate black stone from its hidingplace.

The cool silk of aftergrass under her bare feet, the rustle of the poplar leaves, and beyond the blue reaches of the mountain, brought a wildness to her blood as she came back through the meadows, the black stone in her hand, thick and round at its centre, tapering to delicate points at both ends, the flowing rasp of it in his hand against blue steel. She passed a haycock in the old meadow and there the madness took shape. She started to roll the stone up its side, catching it as it fell. Up and down the slack rope she rolled it with excited hands, playing at the edges that turn a child's day to tragedy, until she rolled it quite over the cock. She might have still caught it coming down the other side if she'd rushed round but she stood frozen as it went out of sight.

She inched round after it had fallen, and there it lay in two across a hooftrack, the stone paler where it had broken. I like to imagine she spent many hours in the mountains as she lay in that room. If I believed in a hell or heaven I would believe that God was formed from the First Memory.

The blows that ring on no steel but cause the heart to race in terror before it tires into acceptance.

The night nurse changed with the day and the door of the room was closed even for the Rosary, which Bridget led when my aunt wasn't there.

Always the confident dedication had been, "We offer up this Holy Rosary for the quick recovery of the children's mother," and then a night my aunt had come from town it changed with a nervous catch of the breath, "We offer up this Holy Rosary to almighty God that His will be done."

There was the chair and cold cement of the floor and racing terror tiring into bewilderment.

Crazy word came Sunday from my father. The house was to be cleared the next morning. The deathroom alone was to be left alone and necessary pails and cutlery and pots. The children and maid with the beds and rest of the furniture were to move to the barracks. Owing to pressure of duty he couldn't come but he was sending men and a lorry. She would die alone with the nurses.

After the word came the whole world was arrested around the leaving in the morning and it was with surprise that the morning came much as any morning, waking into the shiver of its first light and the unbelief that this day would be the end of what had gone on for long.

Her cousin the priest came at eight, the pyx that held the wafer he would place on her tongue a gold gleam in his hand as he climbed the stairs.

Michael my uncle came saying May would be out later but till noon she had no one to mind the sweet shop.

The lorry came at ten, a red lorry with crates, the dust of the coal it usually carried on its crates and in cracks of the floor.

The driver and a helper got out of the cab and the driver handed Michael a note, "It just says he's sorry he couldn't come because of duty." Michael swore under his breath and put the note in his pocket to give to his sister to read. "I suppose we better make a start so," he said as Maggie the maid shouted at the child Margaret who was chasing the cat with tongs.

I stayed out of the house by the lorry; by staying out of the house I could distance myself from the empty spaces each minute left and watch the wardrobes and table and old chairs and the teachests with their fringe of silver fill the front of the lorry.

"Our father didn't come?" I asked the driver with the gravity of a small gentleman.

"No. He couldn't get off," he said and I nodded comprehendingly.

I watched a horse and cart go by on the road, crush of stone yielding to the iron. I watched the cinders of the path, the fallingdown wooden paling of the garden in which she'd never planted the roses she'd planned, the barbed wire about the apple saplings to protect them from the goats, the glass, the trees against the distant blue, feel of the heat on the hot metal of the lorry to shut out of mind the increasing empty spaces within that brought me closer to the room upstairs and what I could not face.

Up and down the wooden stairs the feet went.

"Easy does it. Wait till I just get a better grip. A few inches this way," the lorry was filling, one of the rooms completely empty.

The window of the sickroom opened. Nurse McCaffrey's dark head beckoned and in a low voice called, "Your mother's been asking for you."

I looked at her with masked hatred but walked, cement of the floor, stairs, past the rooms empty except for the stripped beds. I held the loose brass knob of the door without pushing and as in a dream I was in the room, priest and nurse by the bed.

A shadow was to fall forever on the self of my life from the morning of that room, shape it as the salt and wind shape the trees the tea lord had planted as shelter against the sea, for in the evenings they do not sway as other trees in the cooling wind, but stay stubbornly bent away from their scourge the sea, their high branches stripped of bark and whitened, and in the full leaf of summer they still wear that plumage of bones.

"There's no way out of it. They've rusted too much in the damp. We'll just have to hammer the sections apart," I heard.

"If that bloody man was only halfnatural and left the house as it was for a time," our uncle muttered and the driver answered in an apologetic tone, "Everything else is in the lorry except these beds."

"I suppose there's nothing for it but to hammer them loose," and the nurse hurried to close the door I'd left open on the voices. "I'll go down and look for hammers," were the last words.

The priest sat by her head. A wan smile played in her eyes and on the parchment lips. She held me still in her eyes.

"The lorry'll be going soon, mother."

"Not for a little time yet," the pale lips moved but she held me still in her eyes.

"I came to say goodbye, mother," the priest had a hand on my shoulder as I bent to kiss her, and as lips touched everything was burned away except that I had to leave at once. If I stayed one moment longer I was lost. Panic was growing: to put arms about the leg of the bed so that they'd not be able to drag me away, to stay by that bed forever.

"Goodbye, mother."

I had to turn and walk, get out of that room.

"You picked a good day for leaving," Michael put his hand on my hair as he went into the bedroom with hammers.

The beating apart of the beds rang through the house, rusted at the joinings by damp; the thin walls shivered at each beat, and the picture of the Sacred Heart swayed on its cord.

"Kate, Kate," I heard the priest's voice calming her between the strokes.

"If only that man was halfnatural and left it till after," Michael swore as he beat the beds apart, the solid beating giving way to a lighter clanging as the parts fell free.

"We're nearly finished now," the driver said as the last beats rang, and when they stopped the unnatural silence was filled by the priest's murmurs from the deathroom. Hurriedly they took the sections downstairs and stood them against the sides of the lorry. The lorry was full now except for Maggie and the children.

"Will it be going soon?" I pestered the driver.

"Soon I think."

"If you turn that knob what happens?"

"That knob? The indicators come out."

The yellow indicators were lit when they came out and why would the lorry not move and end this tugging ache. Ache to go up the stairs and drink in her pale face in its pillow of hair. The window of her room seemed to stare at me. Though how could I stand the horror of a second leavetaking? I'd not be able to leave, and they'd have to drag me away.

"Why doesn't the lorry go?"

The door opened and was left open. Michael came out, the girl children with their dolls, and Maggie with the cancer child my brother in her arms. Girl by girl was lifted by Michael into the back of the lorry and I climbed up glad to have anything to do to escape the eye of the window.

"Sit on the mattresses," Michael said as he lifted up the backboard and dropped the pins in. Maggie was to ride in the cab with the men.

The engine started. The rocking of the furniture kept my eyes from the window as the lorry crawled up the cinders to the road. Furniture lurched dangerously on the road but was held by the ropes. As it gathered speed we put hands through the crates to comb the rushing air with fingers.

Immaculate in his blue uniform, the highcollar unhooked on a bare throat and the whistle chain loose, he was waiting for us by the nettingwire with Mullins and Mrs. Mullins when the lorry got to the barracks.

"Outside the fact that I can afford to take no more leave," he explained awkwardly, for they knew it to be the lie that it was, "I find it too harrowing to see her the way she is now and thought it'd be bad for the children to be there at the end."

He would not go to her bedside but he wept as he lifted each of us in turn towards his mouth. The two women started to sob as Mrs. Mullins took the baby from Maggie. Mullins helped the men loosen the ropes and to take things in and upstairs. As they beat the sections of the iron beds together again some of the children noticed the strokes giving back echoes in the empty rooms and started to shout to listen to their voices echo back. I wasn't able to keep eyes away from Mrs. Mullin's bare legs; how bleached the hairs were above the tennis shoes, the soft pale flesh to the knees and I took a coin and rolled it to see higher into her thighs.

The big kitchen was full of the oppressive silence of his sewing when the word came. He had his back to the window so that the evening light from Oakport fell over his shoulder on the holes he made with the little yellow awl in the leather, the air sharp and resinous with the black wax he used to tease the hempen threads. He held the awl in his teeth as he pulled each stitch tight, and wore a brown apron to protect his uniform.

In this silence the ringing of the telephone behind the closed door of the dayroom echoes up the long hallway. He paused in his sewing to listen but bent again over the boot as Mullins picked up the phone. When the door of the dayroom opened he paused again and sat tensely waiting. The whole room hung still on the heavy boots tolling up the cement. To the timid knock he called, "Come in."

"There's a personal call for you, sergeant."

"Is it from Aughoo?"

"Tis," Mullins nodded glumly.

He undid the knot on the brown apron and left it with the awl and boot on the sewing machine under the window.

"Is it?" Maggie asked as the steps went down the hallway

and when Mullins nodded she burst into tears. I fell into a panic and could not hold the tears back, but it was not certain yet.

In the sobbing his voice on the phone came through the open doors but not what he said. For two or three minutes that seemed eternities he stood still in the dayroom after he'd put the phone down. His steps came quietly up on the cement. Search his face in the doorway: it was true, it could not be true.

"The children's mother died at a quarter past three today," it was true. "May the Lord have mercy on her soul."

He was at the door in his blue uniform, the silver buttons glittering, and he was saying, "The children's mother died at a quarter past three today."

"I'm sorry, sergeant. May the Lord have mercy on her," Mullins made the sign of the cross.

"Go and see when McGeady will be ready with the car: and phone compassionate leave in for me."

"I'll see McGeady first," Mullins was glad to get out of the room.

"I'll need my plain suit and there should be a black tie in the bottom drawer of the wardrobe," he said to Maggie, whose breasts shook with convulsive sobbing. "First we'll offer the Holy Rosary up for the repose of her soul."

He took the cloth purse from his pocket. The beads spilled into his palm. He put a newspaper down and knelt with both elbows on the table, facing the big mirror, a withered palm branch high in its ornamental fretwork.

"Thou O Lord wilt open my lips," he began and paused when it was only answered by Maggie's sobbing, and low giggles of the girls.

"And my tongue shall announce Thy praise," he had to make the response when none came, very sternly, staring fixedly into the mirror.

"We offer up this Rosary to Almighty God that He may grant to the children's mother's soul eternal rest in heaven."

So she was gone, she would not move to any word or call;

in her brown habit facing the plywood wardrobe she would lie quite horribly still; her raised feet would not sway or stir to any touch or fingers, her eyes would be closed, her white beads twined in her fingers, the wedding gold and the engagement ring with its one stone missing gone. O but if only I could have had back then that whole hour I had wasted down with the lorry on the cinders so that I could see her stir or smile. I would portion the hour out so that I would see her forever. She must have felt that I too had abandoned her in the emptying of the house and the horrible beating apart of the iron. Not one moment of that hour could be given back and it was fixed forever that I would not watch with her while the house was being emptied. I had not loved her enough.

He paused ominously in front of the big mirror. The girls were giggling to one another through the lattices of their fingers.

"Can no respect be shown to the dead or do I have to enforce respect?"

They were frightened and at once the laughter changed to imitative weeping.

"Crying isn't respect. The respect she needs now is prayer," he said towards the mirror and somehow the shambles was struggled through to the last amen.

Maggie poured hot water for his shaving and then went upstairs to get out his plain clothes. He'd finished shaving when she came down to tell him his clothes and black tie were ready. Mullins's boots came on the cement.

"McGeady will be round in a minute, as soon as he changes into his good clothes. Is there anything else I can do?" Mullins reported.

"No. Nothing else."

There was nothing different about him when he came down except the black tie and he carried his gaberdine coat on his arm as usual. McGeady's car was waiting at the gate. He did not blow the horn as he would on a court day. Our father then gave Maggie some money and slowly and self-consciously kissed each of us in turn as he left. We watched the small blue

Vauxhall until it went out of sight at Lavin's Hill.

There was the feeling that life couldn't be as this after he'd gone, fear of any word or move; and this was broken by the coming of the women. *The poor children*, broke me as completely as I had feared I'd be broken if I had stayed longer in the room the day the lorry left and there was no leg of bed to try to hold on to, for now she was gone, it no longer mattered to where they took me, she would not be there. The first rush was to cross the rhubarb beds to the stink of the lavatory in the heat but even that was too open. It was better in the darkness under the stairs, where the bags of old socks and ravelled sweaters were kept, and it was totally dark when I bolted the small door. I opened one of the bags far in under the stairs and put my face into the old wool and camphor and for the first time started to weep purely.

She was gone where I could not follow and I would never lay eyes again on that face I loved. If I could only have that wasted hour by the lorry back to drink in that face, if I had it now, one moment of it, to go up those stairs, and look on her one more last time.

Her feet, her brown shoes on the dust of the road as we walked under the rookery for a can of milk that late August evening after we'd come from the barracks at the end of the school holidays.

Tired wrists holding the ream of wool for her that she was winding into a ball, between us the winter fire leaping, the winding that seemed it would go on forever.

She hands me her bag on our way to school to turn aside to vomit into the nettles. Green plums she must have eaten.

It was all gone now and I could not even grasp that wasted hour with her when they beat the beds apart. What must she have felt when the lorry left.

I heard them calling my name. "Was he seen down by the river?" and it was easier to come out.

"Your mother will be up in heaven looking down on you," a woman said as she forced me to take some tea, one of those busy out of idleness, they must always bring us the mirror of our grief.

"Are any of them to be let go to the funeral?" I heard them ask.

"No. He said not."

"It's much better for them to remember her as she was in life."

Night came on so slow that it seemed it would never come. The women started to leave for their own houses. If only I could get to Aughoo and climb the stairs then I would be certain and there'd be less pain.

"Do you think are we likely to be sent for?" I asked Maggie.

"No. I don't think so. You better go to bed now to be up for First Mass tomorrow."

Waking into the summer morning, the yew tree in gentle sway outside the window and the stone walls running towards the church in its shelter of evergreens, and the unreal memory that yesterday she died.

"Can I stay at home from Mass today?"

"What respect is that to the dead?"

"I don't feel well."

"You'll have to go, and that's the end all, what would the people think?"

It was hard to pass the men along the chapel wall, run the gauntlet of their eyes *his mother is dead*, the recognition making it unendurable. There was safety in the anonymity of the benches until the priest took a slip of paper from his breviary before the sermon and read, "Your prayers are requested for the soul of Kate Moran, wife of Sergeant Moran, who passed from this life yesterday. For those of the parish wishing to attend, her body will be removed to Aughoo church at six this evening and the burial will take place at . . ."

I felt put under a blowlamp, skin stripping, panic to escape but I was hemmed in by men. Announcements were always for others. It was for my mother they were praying. My mother would be taken to the church at six and at three tomorrow she would be buried.

I ran from the church at the first break in the men when Mass was over, leaping the stone walls off the road as soon as I got to Gilligan's field, and reached the shelter of the barracks before the cars and bicycles and hatted women. I had to be out of their sight.

All day people trickled to the still house in my mind. Down the cinder path they'd come, shake hands at the door, "I am very sorry for your trouble," climb the stairs to look on her face a last time, the living face I had a whole hour to look on and threw away. They'd kneel at the foot of the bed, watched by the woman who had taken over the night vigil, and they'd have tea or wine or whiskey when they'd come down while they talked a last time of the life she had on this earth. As she lay cold in the light of the candles she'd never move or smile again.

All day I watched the clock. At six they'd take her to the church.

Once the hands passed five I grew feverish as I pictured the house. The brown coffin would come in the glass of the hearse. People would leave the house and gather outside as soon as they looked in the empty coffin. The door would be shut, the blinds of the windows drawn.

On chairs beside the bed the coffin would rest while my father and those close to her knelt to look on her a last time and why could I not kneel to look on her face a last time too.

They'd lift her from the bed, a feather; and place her in the wood. Quietly they'd turn the screws of the lid. Never in this world would her face be seen again. The chanting of prayer from the people kneeling on the earth outside would rise as they carried her down, past the rooms empty of furniture, awkwardly in hands down the stairs; but once outside, the coffin would ride on the living shoulders up the cinders to the open door of the hearse, bareheaded men and blackscarved women timidly chanting the litany in the open day.

The hearse would move slow, they had not far to go to the church on the road rich with the whitethorns at the end of May, past the pool where the creamery horses drank, over the railway bridge and the blinds of Mahon's shop drawn, the coffin sloping in the glass as it climbed uphill to the school, pausing at the school where she had taught, the minute bell from the church tolling clear.

All night they'd leave her before the high altar, under the red sanctuary lamp, candles in tall black candlesticks about the coffin; they'd leave her there all night in the brown coffin, the church empty, the doors locked and the coffin in that horror of stillness beneath the lamp, but at least she was not in the earth yet, somehow it might be all turned back yet.

A pale mist of morning gave way to a blazing noon, bright gashes of wheels on the tar of the main road, dust puffing on the dirt road as I watched people gather at the bridge to pack into three cars. They were going to the funeral.

I watched the hands of the clock jerk to two, an hour before three, as long as the hour I had lost on the cinders, trying to keep pictures of her in the days of her life as the minutes remaining to her above clay beat away. At ten to three I was frantic. I looked that no one was looking and took the blue clock from the sideboard and weeping stole with it out to the avenue to move in the shade of the evergreens, the flat and fragrant elder blossom at the gap that she'd never watch turn to clusters of small black grapes again, and close to the great oak I hid in the deeps of Lenehan's laurels to hold the cold glass of the clock to my face as it beat out the last minutes to three. I gave a low cry but could not stop the steel blue hands. A wren flitted from branch to bare branch under the leaves, and the church was filling, bicycles stacked against the wall, the old bell on the grass. They'd genuflect on the flagstones. They'd see the candles lit about the coffin. The hand gave a last jerk to three. I could stop nothing now. The altar boys in scarlet and white come with the vessels and cross and sit on the steps after the priests have sat on the chairs by the side of the rail. My father and uncles move to the table outside the gate of the altar and the men file up to leave silver on the green of the table, my father and uncles counting the silver into blue bags, clink of silver in the coughing silence of the church, and when it is all counted they hand the little bags to the priests with a small piece of paper telling the sum. Canon Glyn goes with the slip of paper to the centre of the altar and reads out the sum, and praises the departed for as long as the sum is large. The clock in my hands stuttered out the time as it passed in the shade of the laurel.

They come through the gate to bless the coffin, the boys holding the smoking thurible, the holy water to hand to the priest, a boy with the cross on high. She has waited for the Lord as sentinels wait for the dawn, and now she goes to the Lord; but the Lord has many servants, and I had but the one beloved. The clock beat in my hands in the shade of the laurels as I cried. The candles smoke as they are quenched and put aside. My father and uncles struggle as they raise the coffin to their shoulders, the cross moving ahead, and the crowd follow behind the coffin that rides a last time on living shoulders; it moves from the porch out into the sunlight, its brass glittering, swaying a little as the bearers change step on the gravel. Slowly it moves round the sacristy past Dolan's gate to where there's a gash of fresh clay, among the crosses and flowers. They have lined the grave with moss so that the coffin will go softly down on the ropes. The crowd circle the grave, the priest's ceremonial clay falls on the boards, they bow their heads in prayer as the quick shovelfuls thud on the hollow boards. The brown wood is covered. The grave is filled. Green sods are replaced over the clay. The crowd scatter away. I come out of the laurels with the hands of the clock at twenty to four and after the first blindness I see two men come in the avenue. They have fishing rods. They have come to borrow the barrack boat. I forget the clock in my hands as I run to meet them before they get to the gate. I want nothing more than to be with them on the river in the boat.

"You're going out in the boat?"

"We're thinking of giving it an old try anyhow."

"Could I come with you?"

They were at once embarrassed, shuffling, "You know the day that it is?"

"Yes," I admitted reluctantly, "But I don't think it'd be harm to go on the river."

The glittering lake, the calm oar strokes in the shade of Oakport, hands on the bamboo: her funeral was no more now than the exasperation of this obstacle to an evening on the river.

"You know I don't think it'd look good for you to be out in the boat when they got home."

"I don't think they'd mind."

"Ah, give it a miss today. There'll be many other days."

Their feet moved on the stones. I followed them down the long grass of the meadow to the boat in the hope they'd relent.

"By the way, what are you doing with the clock?" one of the men asked as he untied the boatrope.

"I brought it out to look at the time," I was aware for the first time in minutes of the blue clock beating in my hands.

"I'd leave it back in the house if I were you," he said but seeing me turn away called, "There'll be many a day for the river. Maybe next Sunday we'll give it a try."

I heard the rustle of the boat push through the big drowning leaves out into the current. The oars squealed fiercely at the first stroke and there was silence of oars while a can of water was poured over the rowing pins. The strokes were quiet after the pouring as the boat rowed away, the beating of the clock louder in my head than in my hands.

Suddenly they were home from the funeral, three carloads, relatives seeing my father home, my father heavily robed in his sense of his new responsibilities. "The past is with God. We have to still bear our cross as well as we are able," he said solemnly to a commiserating woman relative. Maggie gave them tea and fruitcake. The worst was when they looked at us with moon-eyes over the teacups and said, *The poor children*, causing confusion of wanting at once to strike at them and to break down. I was in awe of them too. They had seen her laid out, they had followed the coffin, they had watched the grave fill, while I had followed it only on the beating clock in the laurels. The child of her cancer slept through it all by the window and when one of the women said, "Isn't it good he can sleep so prettily without ever knowing," I could stand it no longer and left to go down to the river. A terrible new life was beginning, a life without her this evening and tomorrow and the next day and next day forever. If I could only have that wasted hour on the cinders back and could portion it so that I could lay eyes now and again on her face she would not be gone forever. The men came in the boat, they must have caught fish, for the barrack cat was purring out on the stones as they guided the boat in through the drowning leaves. I heard someone calling me for the Rosary before I could see what fish they had. He was kneeling facing the big mirror, his beads in his hands, and he began as soon as I knelt. "In the name of the Father and of the Son and the Holy Ghost. We offer up this Rosary for the soul of the children's mother."

The shadow had fallen on the life and would shape it as the salt and wind shaped the trees the tea lord had planted as shelter against the sea: and part of that shaping lead to the schoolroom of this day, but by evening the life would have made its last break with the shadow, and would be free to grow without warp in its own light.

Part Two

"One day I'd say Mass for her."

Through the sacrifice of my life to the priesthood I'd redeem the betrayal of her in that upstairs room. For years I promised it to her memory that, "One day I'd say Mass for her." I'd lift the chalice in anointed hands on the altar and in the lonely rooms of presbyteries I'd be faithful to her, but when the time arrived for me to make that sacrifice I failed her once again. I wasn't able to renounce the longing to enter the mystery of the lovely and living flesh of woman, and out of guilt I chose second best. I followed her footsteps to the Training College. In some country school I'd teach out my days. If I was lucky I'd find a girl lovely as she was whom I'd love and live with in the heart of the country. It seems all far away from this last day in the classroom: a confused child's world of guilty dreaming.

They took two years to train us as teachers, each day enclosed between morning Mass and evening Devotions in the chapel before we climbed the stone stairs to our cubicles. Between classes and study and meals we circled the path round the football field in twos or threes or fours talking of women, the old lime trees and high wall between us and the red neon of the Drum Cinema, the growling roar of the distant city. For a few hours we were allowed out Wednesday and Saturday afternoons, and they found us in cinemas. Sunday was the one day we had completely free, though the gates were shut at ten. Sunday afternoon we went to dances, most of the girls at the afternoon dances from the girls' Training College across the city; and towards the end of the two years in one of those girls I found her again.

The queue in Granby Row that warm Sunday afternoon

for the Kingsway, Matt Talbot's altar against the wall, the little wooden kneeler and statue of the Virgin dustcoated and shabby, dustcoated too the glass jars in which fresh daffodils and narcissi stood: old mad Dublin labourer who fell with chains festering in his flesh where we queued to dance.

The doorman in black evening dress tore our tickets in two and we went out of the day into the artificial light of the dancefloor. The band was playing as I entered. The men and women faced each other across an empty floor, where three or four couples, dancers who had gone to dancing schools, were displaying their steps. As the floor gradually filled, those with less confidence took courage. When the floor was filled all dancing was reduced to one happy universal shuffle. As each dance was called there was a charge of men across the floor towards the prettier girls, who'd turn to the plainer sisters of their group with the formal, "Excuse me, please." The girls who hadn't been asked to dance then took step after step of humiliation back to the wall as the ranks about them thinned, before finally sitting down on the long bench to watch out the dance.

"Will you dance, please?" I asked a girl and she nodded and turned to the girls standing with her to say, "Excuse me, please."

"Do you like these dances?" I remember the inane awkwardness of all dancehall conversations.

"Not very much. I hardly ever come."

"Where do you like to dance then?"

"In the holidays. Bundoran."

"You must be near there then?"

She named where she was from. It was in the heart of the mountains from where my mother had come. I could see past the ballroom to the girl with the emery stone in the hayfields on the side of those iron mountains as we jostled our way round the floor. I learned she'd come out of those mountains the same way as she had come by a county scholarship instead of the old King's to the Marist convent in Carrick and on to the girls' Training College in Carysfort.

She started to ask me about my path to the College, which was hardly different from her own.

The quickstep entered its last interval. I grew nervous. I didn't want her to disappear back into the band of girls. I mightn't get to dance with her again.

"Wouldn't you like to have an orange or something with me after the dance?"

"I promised to go back to the girls after the dance."

"You can go back to them after the next dance," my voice stuttered in its anxiety.

"It's not nice to break a promise."

"Whatever you like but I'm sure they won't mind for one dance," I pressed as the music stopped and we faced each other on the floor.

"All right as long as I can go back to them after the next dance," she suddenly relented and my tenseness went.

We drank orange juice on a balcony above the dancing. Over us, between the mock marble arches, hung baskets of plastic flowers. What we spoke were nothings but each nothing was suffused with sweetness and excitement. The dance ended. She moved to cross the floor to rejoin her group of girls. I said, "Why don't you dance the next dance with me? You'd just be back when someone else will ask you."

"But I must then go back after we dance."

"Of course."

We moved in a slow waltz, the lights dimmed to blue. I could feel the ripe softness of her body, look on her lovely and calm face, the sheen of her black hair.

"Are you going to the Dress Dance?" I asked.

"I was thinking of not going, but I haven't made up my mind completely."

"Why don't you come with me?"

"Have you not someone else?" colour came to her cheeks.

"There are people I can take but I'd rather if you came."

"I'll come," she nodded, and I was happy. I'd see her for all those six weeks to the dance.

The waltz ended, she went back to the line of girls, I saw her dance the next dance with someone else. The next dance was a ladies' choice. I was afraid until she came towards me, and we laughed nervously together as she asked me to dance. During the dance we arranged to meet the next Saturday at the Metropole and go to some cinema.

That night after chapel when I'd drawn the curtain of the cubicle, I sat fully dressed on the bed, facing the narrow wardrobe and jug and basin, my hand shading my eyes, in that sweet ecstasy of first love. It seemed that all my life till now had been nothing but a preparation for this day, the first death and its suffering burned away, welded into one desire for this new love, for a life with her, to live in sweet love with her forever.

Saturday came in a drunkenness of anticipation, hairoiling of hair in the mirror, brushing of clothes and shoes till they shone, and the crease of the trousers pressed to a knife-edge.

She let me take her hand in the cinema but went rigid when I put my arm round her shouders. Saturday and Sundays went as this in cinemas and dancehalls and in between I did little but dream. There was a hot Sunday we tried to go to the sea at Howth but the queues for the buses were too long, as she'd to be in by seven: so we went and ate sherbet in a café and listened to the jukebox play. As once there was the security of the coming summer for my love in the upstairs room to get well again so now there was the rock of the coming Dress Dance to give my love the dangerous security to grow.

In an illfitting hired dress suit I met her outside her convent gates with a hired car. She wore a long dress of white taffeta, gathered at the waist, with a small gash of red carnations pinned at her hip. We danced, awkward in the hired suits: we had the included meal: we sat at tables of eight: towards the end of the dance we had the professors, who'd come with their middleaged wives, sign our dancecards: we had our photos taken, she in the long white dress, and I in my straggedly black suit and bow. In some quiet street we kissed in the car afterwards, and I spent long trying to talk her into some way of regularly meeting now that our lives were changed. I argued so long with her that the convent gates were closed when we got back. At first she panicked but was then furious. I persuaded her to climb slowly the bars of the gate and I was able to lift the long dress over the spikes. There was a glimmer of thighs as the folds fell free and she did not speak as she hurried on the gravel towards the closed Gothic door in the summer halflight. I saw her the next day on the train home but she was with other girls and I was unable to be alone with her. She made it quite clear though that she was furious with me over the closed gates.

It was late June and the hayfields, and by brute work it was possible to maim longing, sink dogtired into unconsciousness at night, but Sunday was free, and there was no pleasure in joining a carload to go to one of the carnivals. I cried secretly, and wrote to her that I had been waiting for a letter from her, and would drive down to see her if she'd tell me when.

Our letters crossed: a long letter came from her, which began, *My heart/is a fountain/of sorrow/unspoken.* Whether it was a fountain or not it was certainly spoken. The letter ran to eleven pages. She had come home to find her father in hospital with a nervous breakdown. Apparently what hurt her most was that he'd bought a bicycle for her graduation and wasn't there to give it to her. They'd not told her for fear she'd get upset so close to the examinations. She had been dancing while her poor father who'd bought the bicycle was in hospital. I wrote her by return, I'd drive to her house the following Sunday, I'd get there about three.

I was dismayed when I got to the house at three to find she wasn't there. She was out having a driving lesson. Her mother, tall as she, with the same strong body, but the face turned to granite under the grey hair, met me with folded arms.

"I don't know when she'll be back. She should make it her business to be back if she's invited guests," there was an iron tenacity about her, to wrest a living from near poverty and to push her children out into a better world through the door of education. One day my love may be old and hard as she, I thought.

"I hope your husband is better," I offered out of unease.

"He's much better," she answered and after a pause: "Never touch the drink. It's the ruination of everything."

When finally she returned from driving she answered my reproach, "You weren't here when I came at three," with the careless, "Paddy Joe came round and offered a driving lesson and I went." There was nothing I could say except angrily think of *My heart/is a fountain/of sorrow/unspoken.* She made tea and told the young girl to go to the shop and take a packet of biscuits so as not to have to bother with bread. A look of antagonism passed between mother and daughter but the mother didn't speak. After we'd had the tea I said, "Why don't we leave?"

"Where are you thinking of?"

"We might go to the carnival dance in Carrick."

"I'll have to change out of this frock and sandals."

When she changed I thanked the mother and we left. I tried to quarrel with her in the car but I was only too grateful for my crumb of explanation. All night we danced together, the green canvas of the marquee as becalmed sails in the moonlit summer's night. After the dance she embraced me passionately and combed fingers through my hair and my head was full of dreams as I drove her home. As soon as I stopped outside the house she leaned away from me with her back to the door of the car and said, "You know I am very fond of you but I am certain we should break it off tonight."

"Why?"

"With Daddy in hospital I'll have to look after the others. I've already been offered a place in the local school."

"Will you take it?"

"Yes. I start in a few days."

"That shouldn't make any difference. We could wait. We could see each other as often as we are able."

"No. It's no use."

"Maybe in three or four years we could be married," I pressed.

"No. It'd never come to anything. It's better to break now."

"You don't love me then?"

"I've grown very fond of you, but no, I don't love you. I am not free to love anybody now."

It went on as this, the plea and the rejection. The grey light of day began to filter into the moonlight. Suddenly the door of the house opened and her name was called angrily, several times. "See, it's just like the Dress Dance but thank you for the evening," and she got out and shut the door. I watched her shape climb to her mother's dark shape in the doorway, heard some small stones roll that her shoes dislodged. Both shapes merged, without looking back. The door closed. I looked for some minutes at the blank house and started the engine. I drove slowly, feeling the silence and cold of the morning. As I circled the Lough I saw the lights of Drumshambo shine in their stillness across the sheet of Allen, feeling the horrible heaviness against the energy of twenty years.

She was, at twenty, as are most women, ripe to enter fully into her sexual life: while I, at the same age, was still a child. The same hands that combed through my hair that night are in a classroom in the nineteenth-century mansion a few yards from where I teach out this last day, and she blushes when we meet, but now that we are both ready for a life together it has all changed again. The afternoons at the Kingsway, the dark of the cinemas, the long white dress of taffeta were but as hour-marks on a wall with the paintbrush that measured the change of my longing from her as she lay dying in that upstairs room to a young and lovely woman, about to enter her life. As her mother angrily called her name, and I listened to the small stones her shoes dislodged as she climbed away from me in the cold of the early morning moonlight, the shadow that had fallen so long from the dead now fell from her young life.

I ran from the shadow and the country dream it withered, by way of small town schools, each move bringing me closer to the city, till the wet night I walked under the stripped almond and cherry trees to Maloney's house and was given the job I am to lose this night at eight.

The forgetting was slow and painful and gradual. I

remember finding in an old suit a ticket a photographer had given me as we walked from the Metropole under the pillars of the post office and taking it to the address in a squalid basement in Earl Street. They refused to develop it at first, saying it was too old. I argued it was precious to me, that the person in the photo was now dead and offered to pay them more than the usual price if they'd look it up in their back files. When they found and developed it I was afraid to look at it. I made myself busy with payment to avoid seeing it as they put it in a brown envelope. I crossed the street to Mooney's and after ordering a drink went to the lavatory. With shaking hands I took the photo from the envelope. There was the dear face, the dress she wore in that summer's day, the rich curves of the body under the dress; but the longer I looked at it the more simple celluloid it became and nothing, as the corpse we search for the person that has fled becomes any skin and bones, and I let the photo drop on the floor. We know leaving the house of the dead that the person we came to look on a last time has totally fled us and lives only among the shadows of memory.

The distractions of the city quickened forgetting, the excitement of books for the first time, no longer the dull slog for exams but ways of seeing, one's own world for the first time. The laughter and argument of pubs, and late at night the dances, girls from the dances, and fumbled sex in the back seats of cars or on bedsittingroom sofas or against alley walls, wet trouser legs and the stiff grey stain that had to be sent to the cleaners.

It was Elinor who first taught me the loveact in whatever dignity it has. I met her at a party on the other side of the city and she offered me a bed in her house close by as I was looking for a taxi to take me across the night city.

As we climbed the stairs to the room she'd offered me for the night, I put my hand on her hair and kissed her and she returned the kiss.

"Is the house empty?" I asked.

"Yes. The children won't be back from boarding school for

another four weeks."

"Can I stay with you tonight instead of in the spare room?"

"You want to?"

"Yes." And we went together into her room and kissed.

Without turning on the light we let our clothes drop on the floor and got into the big bed in the corner of the room. Now that I was to spend the whole night naked in a woman's arms I was afraid.

"Don't worry. It'll be all right," she said softly when she felt me tremble. Calmly she offered all her woman's body to my hands and lips and guided me within her. I rested within her as if I could not believe I'd entered the rich dark mystery of a woman's body, this feeling of the rich mystery open all night to me far more than the throb of pleasure. Then she moved me within her. Each hour that night I must have entered her, as if I could not believe that the flower of a woman's body lay open for me by my side all the night.

"Did you get any pleasure, my love?" I asked her in the first light.

"I don't care about that," she smiled. "What is so good is to feel skin again. What is hardest being single after years of marriage is this craving for skin."

She let me feast eyes and hands on her in the light and for me to watch as she opened for me while I went slowly within her before falling on her breasts.

"It is strange to think how frail the chances of the night together was if you go over the party, what a blessed chance it was," I said as I sat by the window in the indescribable happiness of wanting nothing whatever in the world over hot coffee and toast and marmalade.

"I think life is mostly that way. Anything that is given can be at once taken away. We have to learn never to expect anything, and when it comes it's no more than a gift on loan," she added quietly.

For four miraculous weeks we lived together, doing everything that lovers do, without any of the tensions of young lovers. At the end of the four weeks, after we'd come from dancing and there'd been an incident with a drunk over the disparity of our ages, she said as we lay together, "The children will be back from boarding school tomorrow," and I knew with nothing but undying gratitude that this would be the last night I'd enjoy the rich gift of the body she had given to me.

It was that same gift that gave me the confidence to enter several casual and purely sensual affairs and eventually to fall into a calamity of love.

It was in one of the expensive dance halls in the city that we met, with bars and waiters, and where the dancers—especially the men—were seldom very young. She was tall and dark-haired, and there was about her a hard if not cruel gaiety. Her body moved with complete ease and freedom as she danced, her eyes shining with pleasure.

"Which would you prefer, to be in love or to have someone love you?" the early patter went.

"To have someone love me of course," she laughed.

"Can't it be tiresome to have someone love you that you don't want?"

"It's better than being in love."

"What is bad about being in love then?"

"Not being able to think about anything but the other person, not being able to sleep," her face went quiet as she spoke then immediately returned to the gaiety of her dancing.

"Why don't we have a drink and talk?" I asked her as the dance ended. We found an empty table and had the waiter bring us gins and tonics. We drank and danced and talked till almost three and in the car she was as easy and uninhibited as in her dancing, only drawing back at the very last, saying plainly that she was unprepared and it was dangerous but that we would have other times.

Outside the small suburban house where she lived with a married sister we arranged to meet in two nights. "I used to live alone before," she referred to the unhappy love she'd told me about over the drinks at the table, "but then I wasn't able to be alone and moved to my sister's. They were very good to me but now I feel I'd like to live alone again."

I was looking forward to the night we'd meet with a new excitement that is the seed of danger.

The next night we danced again in the same hall. I was afraid that if I changed anything the magic I'd started to feel about the first night might go away, but midway through the dancing she said she was tired—once every so often, nobody ever was able to predict when or why, they had a dreadful day in the office—and we sat twenty more minutes at a table over a drink and I drove her home, kissing her a brief goodnight. We'd meet Saturday in town inside the G.P.O. at seven.

Because I wanted to walk as well as the difficulty of Saturday-night parking I didn't take the car. She was finishing a lettercard at one of the big circular tables inside the G.P.O. and when she'd posted it I asked how she'd like to spend the evening.

"Why don't you decide that this evening?" a mischievous mockery showed in her eyes as she watched me.

"The cinemas have all queues. The dance halls will be crowded and drunken. Why don't we have a quiet night, walk, and have a few drinks in some pub."

"Settled." With the same mocking playfulness she put a mock proprietary arm in my arm and we walked through the Saturday night jostling festival and had three gins in an old pub by the river. Our talk kept returning to some comic incidents of our childish sensuality even though both of us deliberately tried to change to some more adult theme. When the pub started to fill I asked nervously, "It's getting so crowded why don't we buy a bottle of wine or something and go to my place?"

"Right," she smiled with the same mockery. "We can walk. The night is warm."

I drew the faded red curtain and put a match to a fire of coal and wood laid in the grate while she examined the old Victorian bed with its brass spears, the faded red of the cane chairs and the cracked dressing-table mirror, the shelves of books.

"What do you think?" I asked as I put two glasses on the table and uncorked the white wine.

"It's not exactly the Ritz," she giggled as dust came away on a finger she placed on the wardrobe top.

"It's quiet though and no one bothers you."

I turned off the light fixed in the ancient Chianti bottle, for the firelight now flamed on the wallpaper and more softly on the long curtain. She came and sat on my knee in the big chair, reaching now and then for the glass of white wine she'd put on the mantel above the fire as I slowly and awkwardly undid the buttons of her blouse, unhooked her brassière. She moved her mouth on mine as the small breasts fell free to gleam in the flickering light. I kissed the dark nipples in turn before we rose and slipped out of our clothes.

Slowly the hands treasured their knowledge of her body; and far more than my own pleasure was the excitement of feeling her search towards her pleasure and when she reached it turn away from me, her breath catching at a cry, before slowly and firmly coming back to my lips. Several times we made love, each time more freely, and in between we sipped the white wine and watched the firelight flame on the walls. Once I got up to put coal on the fire and she slipped into my overcoat to go to the bathroom outside the door.

Close to five as we parted a last time she said she must go at once and pulled back the clothes.

"But you haven't to go to work tomorrow. You can stay till morning and we can have breakfast together."

"No. I must go now." I saw she'd completely made up her mind.

"I'll drive you then."

"No. I'll get a taxi."

"I'll walk you down to the rank."

"No. It's easier this way," she was already dressed and reaching for her handbag.

"When will I see you next?"

"When do you want?"

"Tomorrow."

"No. It can't be tomorrow.

"Monday is all right?"

"At eight in the G.P.O.," and she was gone. I heard her feet go down the stairs and the click of the Yale lock as she stealthily closed the outside door. I wondered at the suddenness of her going and for the first time the room with the fire blazing seemed curiously useless and empty before I fell into a drained sleep.

We spent many nights in that small room, in the silken cool of skin turning to the sweat and sexual smells of our straining bodies while the firelight flickered on the wallpaper, but always she rose and left before daybreak. As the better weather arrived we drove to hotels in the country, but even there she insisted we take single rooms. "But why?" I asked. "That's the why. I won't stay otherwise," she smiled her hard enigmatic smile, and I did not press her further. In these single rooms she put no restraint on our lovemaking which grew to wantonness of mouth and glycerine; but towards four or five her beautiful shoulders would rise on one arm and she'd ask, "Do you want to go to the other room or will I?" "All right I'll go." I'd dress hurriedly and kiss her as she turned towards sleep. Sometimes I'd protest but was secretly glad of the cool and peace of the empty morning room and fresh linen after the savagery of the lovemaking. Once only did she draw closer to me, an evening in O'Connell Street, the day done and people already hurrying under the neon to cinemas and theatres but the street still full of the gentle lingering glory of the sun, and she turned to me a face vivid with the beauty of its excitement and said, "If I was married and had two children I would envy no single girl no matter how beautiful she was;" and while I saw the direction she was leading, what I had with her was already too perfect for me to want to change. When I did not follow her, leaving her words hang idle in the busy street, I saw her face harden as she quickened her walk.

As candles on a table are instinctively lit before sitting to a meal, I went to light the small fire of paper and sticks and coal in the grate of the room at the end of that evening when she said, "What do you want to do that for? The night is hot enough." After the first touches she stridently rose above me on both hands, watching greedily back to where she moved the mound of soft hair in and out on the rod. "Harder," she whispered as I pulled at the nipples with fingers and teeth, the beautiful body gleaming as cold as if it was an enamelled fish above me; and she did not cry that it hurt, but fell panting on me so that I had to put arms around as she ground her bone on mine. It hurt, and so cold and passionate at once that I had to imagine other nights of love to keep my desire alive. Her cry was more of anger than of pleasure when she came and I had to hold her in my embrace or she would have freed herself before I came. When we did draw apart she rose and dressed quickly and left though it was hardly midnight.

All our loving after was as hard as that evening or made casual by the boredom she made no attempt to conceal. She began to put all kinds of obstacles in the way of our meeting: she had to meet an old schoolfriend who'd come up from the country or help some girl pick a wedding outfit. She laughed at my jealously but I was content with any sexual contact, no matter how cruel or how casual, that would allay my anxiety for a time. My fear of her answering, "Yes," if I asked, "Do you think will we be married?" changed to a fear she'd say, "No," and what contact I was desperately trying to keep with her might cease completely. Years before I had started evening classes at the university, more to pass the evenings and because some friends were doing the same than for any desire of improvement. I had done well enough at the B.A. to be allowed to continue to a Master's and I who had taken it all casually till then started to study long hours into the night. I felt if I got a brilliant degree I would become more attractive to her and our relationship would go back to what it had been in the beginning except this time we'd marry. She showed no interest in the long paper I handed in but she promised to meet me the evening the written examinations finished.

I have done well, I thought as I walked that evening away

from the examination hall; she will love me. The Green was in full leaf, red splashes of the geraniums in the beds, and bodies stretched out on deck-chairs along the walks. She is waiting for me in the dark cool of Mooney's, I thought as I crossed the Bridge, the Japanese cherry that earlier I had watched blossom by the water's edge as I went to and from lectures now in leaf, we will have drinks and go to dinner in some restaurant, and spend a long night of love and the longer rest of our lives together.

She was waiting at a table in the corner of the empty bar. Her arms were bare. She had a mustard-coloured dress and sandals and a scarf of pale silk and dark glasses. The door of the silent bar was open on the street.

"It's over," I smiled on her.

"That must be a relief," she said. Her voice was cold.

I went to the counter and got the dry sherry she wanted and a cold Lager, wondering why she had not asked how I had done.

"There's something I have to tell you that's not easy," she said as soon as I put the drinks down and I wanted to see her eyes behind the dark glasses.

"What?"

"That we should stop seeing each other."

"But why?" suddenly the evening of drinks and dinner and the night and much more was falling around me.

"I am wasting your time by us going out together."

"You're not wasting my time. I don't want to look for anybody else."

"We're wasting both our times. That's what I am trying to say."

"I thought that after a while we'd be married."

"No. It's not possible."

"But why? We've had marvellous times together. We could have a whole life like that together."

"No. You may think that now but it wouldn't work."

"Why not?"

"Your friends for instance could never be my friends."

"I don't care about my friends. You'd come before my friends."

"No. It could not be."

"But why?"

"I am very fond of you but I do not love you. I waited till the examinations were over to tell you. I didn't want to upset you before the exams."

"You have someone else then?" I accused.

"That's neither here nor there."

"How is it neither here nor there?"

"It would make no difference to what I am saying whether there was or not."

The thinstemmed sherry glass was empty. She began to pull on the long white gloves that had lain by her handbag on the table.

"Will you not have one more drink?" I was desperate.

"You stay and have another drink," she had risen.

"Could we not stop seeing each other say for a month and then think about it?"

"No. It won't change in a month."

"How can you be certain?"

"The only reason I waited this long was for the exams to be over."

I came with her through the open door of the bar, without thinking about the barman behind his empty counter.

"Is there no hope at all?"

"I'm very grateful for all the good times you gave me and I'll always be fond of you."

"Couldn't we try again?"

"No. It's better this way. It'd be no use," her voice was very firm.

"Can I not even see you to the house?"

"No. I'm not going to the house."

She was impatient waiting for the bus and hailed the first empty taxi that came down Grafton Street.

She turned her face away as I tried to kiss her as she got into the taxi and gave me instead her gloved hand. Her lips moved.

behind the glass as she gave the driver directions and the pale silk of the scarf about her hair glowed a moment in the back of the taxi before it was lost in the traffic.

I turned mechanically back towards Mooney's but at the corner changed and crossed into Duke Street—not away from any imaginary blood or vomit about the table where we'd sat—but in the heartpause or numbness her going had left I was instinctively drawn to some totally strange place that held no part of our lives together. The bar was old, with wooden partitions along the counter; and I lifted the glass from the worn wood and somehow managed to smile and answer the whitehaired barman's, "Great spell of weather we're having," as he gave me change with, "Great. We can only hope it keeps up." Another customer rattled his glass at the far end of the counter and I was grateful he had to interrupt his wiping round my glass on the counter that might have led on to further conversation. As he moved I was able to sip quietly at the cold beer, stare at the bottles and mirrors, while a voice far away in my head kept mechanically repeating, *So she is gone. It is all over. She will never come back. It has happened all over again.*

The beer didn't even touch the numbness and I thanked the whitehaired barman and started to walk, not in any particular streets but for the blind sake of walking. As I walked and walked in the warm evening one last lecherous longing grew: to strip with her a last time in the room with the fire flickering on the walls, lie on her hard breasts, suck her mouth to mine, sink so deep within her flesh that the bones ground, and as the seed exploded so would the brains within the skull, and I would be free at last, for this terrible longing for her body was death without the oblivion given to the dead. The streetlights came on in the late summer's evening and I still walked, what hair were her lips touching now, what room enclosed her laughter, across what chair was her mustard-coloured dress draped, and I had to get through this night and the next day and the next night, and each of them seemed an eternity long.

No sleep would come later in the room and I lay on the eiderdown and I watched the window grow light and tried to row the two miles of river I had grown up on over again in my mind: using the oar as a pole to push the boat out past the stone wall with the rusted barbed wire hanging from the bleached post, the banks of sallies, wedge of whiterock jutting from McCabe's hillside out into the lake, the black navigation pan and the red above their dark conifer of stone, the burned-down coachhouse of Oakport against the woods, and the gulls rising angrily from the rocks of their little island ringed with reeds as the boat drew close, stroke after whorling stroke: but these calming images would be suddenly pushed out of mind by a frenzy of desire to seize her mouth and thighs and end it all in one last fierce kiss.

The morning gradually filled the window, and the din of birds from the ragged backgarden never seemed so loud. I was grateful for the small despised acts of morning: to change into school clothes, to shave, to comb hair, to walk down the stairs, to wait passively for the bus. I gave the children written work, not able to concentrate enough to teach, or to stay physically still, the small faces watching me suspiciously as I paced restlessly between the desks. No knock fortunately came on the door that morning and no one noticed I ate nothing for lunch. Only Maloney came in the afternoon, twenty minutes or so before the last bell. "What do you have on the *clar, a mhaistir*?" his voice was solicitous, but the face puckered, sensing at once that no work was going on. "Geography, *a mhaistir*, but I've just given them some written work. I don't feel well," desperation gave the explanation a careless authority. "Maybe you'd like to go home, *a mhaistir*? I'd take over till the bell," his natural kindness mingled with his horror of an idle class. "It's just a headache. It'll be all right till the bell, but thanks, *a mhaistir*." "I know you're not one of those teachers who takes a day off every chance they get but there's no use straining too much in the opposite direction—and you don't look well." "Thanks, *a mhaistir*. It's just probably a headache from the last of the exams yesterday." "How did it go?" he was at once full of interest. "Fairly well, I think." "There's nothing I like to see better than a young teacher furthering his education, even though we may lose you to the Inspectorate or the university." "There's little fear of that," I answered. "Just let them work there quietly, *a mhaistir*. It'll be soon the bell. A glass of hot milk and a good night's sleep will work wonders," and smiling he bowed himself out, without any exhortation to the class, and I was grateful and felt less need to pace between the desks after he had gone.

It was in the warm evenings that the torture grew fine: along what seafront, a scarf binding her hair against the evening wind, was she walking hand in hand with her new lover; in what bar were they mingling memories of their previous lives; in what room was he caressingly unbuttoning her dress, she kissing his neck as his trembling hands drew the elasticized silk, and did she open her thighs to him with that low provocative laughter. The torture grew to hatred: if I could see her and kill her at least her power to torture would be stilled, and no jail or shame could be worse than what I was going through; but instead of finding a gun and waiting about her house till she came home in the night, I wrote her a pleading letter: was there chance perhaps she might change her mind and we could begin again? I was easier since the letter was in the postbox, and even happy when some days went by without answer—that she didn't reply at once meant she was giving it serious thought, I lulled myself—and just before I could begin to think she wasn't going to answer at all the blue envelope with the familiar writing and scent fell through the letterbox. I had taken to feverishly watching each delivery move from door to door on the road and I seized it as it fell on the mat and tore it open and rushed through the words to discover the message and it was *No*. Slowly I reread: there was no hope; she didn't want to tell me before, but she had to now, she was going to be married to the man she nearly married before we met. She had only happy memories of our times together, and wished me as much happiness in my future life as she hoped I would want to wish her in her life.

A kind of calm came over me as I read and reread the letter. It was over now. It had at least the comfort of that finality. I was left alone with my own life. I could begin to think from there at least even as I cried against it, "Why should it have to be so?"

The mind—the old sentinel—counselled that in one year or two what I then felt would be totally obliterated; and she, whom I desired to the exclusion of everything else in the world, would come to mean so little that the sight of her crossing the street would give rise to little more than idle curiosity. While I was able to admit that this would all probably come true, it was not truth or philosophy I wanted, but an end to the torment, and she who could end it I could not have. In the meantime I admitted I was ill, drank and ate carefully, kept regimental hours, and even rose to the hypocrisy of writing to thank her for her note, saying that on reflection I completely agreed with her that our relationship could never come to anything more serious, and wished her every success and happiness in her marriage, getting malicious satisfaction as I read through the concoction that it gave no hint of her power. Brooding over why she and no other—even others more abstractly beautiful—should embody that power, I had begun to suspect that what I was experiencing was not the losing of her but the loss of my own life.

Through that current of carnal attraction I had little by little embellished her with everything of myself, made her voluptuous and resplendent with all the images dear to me, made her the custodian of a fantasy of my own life. So as she withdrew, when effecting a simple date with her for an evening of dancing or cinema or drink became difficult, those images dear to me, memories of nights of pleasure, distanced then by the difficulty of seeing her at all, were multiplied and animated a thousand times. I saw her as the priceless and unique and irreplaceable being each person is, but which normally we feel only ourselves to be. I could seek pleasure in her body and no other, in the same way as I could not want to find myself in any body other than my own. The morning of the hammering apart of the sections of the iron beds in the upstairs room, the more gentle night of the dead end of the moonlit road over Allen, grew clear: they were times when my own gradual death, which usually passes unnoticed in the normal drudgery of the days, was made present by the torture of the loss of the self I had imaged on to the other. The actual death—whether it came suddenly or by slow decay—could be very little set beside this imagined death, her shining body the oasis of fruit and shade and water I tried uselessly to draw to my thirsting lips to give life to the life I felt to be reeling about on the sand.

The exam results dropped through the same letterbox as her final letter, and I read them much as I had read her letter. They were better than I had ever hoped. I smiled bitterly after I had put them down, for surely they were withered flowers, since she whom they were intended to please had gone out of my life; but I contented myself by thinking that since all life was stupidity never to have acted stupidly amounted to never having lived at all; and I determined to turn them to my advantage.

One of the symptoms of my illness, or even more possibly the sign of my recovery from it, was if I glimpsed a dress or coat she used wear or a tall figure with dark hair in the street I'd at once start to follow it through the crowds, as children and old people will burn themselves by throwing paraffin on fires in the fascination of flame; and while I followed the movement of the coat or hair through the crowd I was at the same time in terror that the face would turn round and it would be her face. Often turning a corner I would come on a shop window where we had loitered before the opening of some picture house or dance hall and at once the everyday world I was trying to rebuild without her would be devastated by the world I had lost. Everything in the city where it seemed we'd been so happy seemed to exist in order to remind me of her. I thought that if I could only move to some other city where we'd never been together how easier it would be, and I decided to use the exam result to apply for a leave of absence. Maloney was naturally suspicious at first but after I had coated the application with such large phrases as *the modern need to acquaint oneself with other educational systems in order to have a keener appreciation of our own and if I didn't seize the chance now before I settled down it would never come my way again*, he said he'd support it, and to my surprise volunteered to put it personally to Father Curry, the Manager. A day or two later he came smiling into the classroom, "I think it'll be all right, *a mhaistir*. Father Curry grumbled a bit but he'll agree all right, except you know we mustn't seem to push him in case he'd suspect it wasn't all his own doing." "Do you think will we have any difficulty finding a good substitute?" I asked, knowing that if my leaving weakened the school in any way in the headmaster's mind I'd never get away. "It's as if it was planned," he rubbed his hands with pleasure. "The day after we talked I rang this old friend of mine up. He's had to retire this year—lived for teaching—and he'd love to teach here the year you're on leave. You don't have to concern yourself about it. I'll arrange everything."

"I could leave at the end of the month then?"

"Of course we have to wait for Father Curry to say yet but I can see nothing in your way by then."

I was walking on the concrete a few days later with the bell, the brass tongue in my hand, as I had walked with it a last time this morning, when I saw the small stout figure of the priest amble along the iron railings to the school gate. I went to meet him. He put his hand as familiarly on my shoulder now as I had watched him place it on the headmaster's shoulder outside the church the day he consented to my appointment.

"My friend," he said in his goodnatured slothful way.

"Are you keeping well, Father?"

"As well as can be hoped, I suppose, with this ulcer. God forgive me what I'd like to call it," our usual playground conversation had begun line perfect.

"It'd limit you, as far as I can see, that there's nothing you'd be able to eat or drink if you heeded everything those bowsies of doctors told you."

"I suppose they're inclined to exaggerate on the side of strictness."

"Shure, listen," slow pained irritation crossed his suddenly concentrated face, "if you abided by everything they told you, putting it plainly, you might as well be dead. I'll have my glass of Powers Gold Label every night and I won't spoil it with hot milk and I'll have my half bottle of claret with the Sunday roast no matter what they say. If a man has his few harmless pleasures taken away from him what has he to live for? He'll be dead far quicker than the ulcer will kill him. I've given up listening to those bowsies long ago."

"Mr. Maloney told me he mentioned to you my application for a leave of absence?" I ventured.

"Oh yes. You want to go away for a year. What do you want to go away for? Isn't there everything you want in this country?"

I mumbled something about contrasting different educational systems before attempting my doctorate.

"Oh yes. Your headmaster told me how well you did for your degree but if you leave now for a year I'll have the trouble of finding someone to replace you."

"Mr. Maloney says he already has someone suitable, Father."

"Well, if he says that I suppose it's all right. I'll write the letter to the Department tonight but mind you don't get any foolish ideas into your head while you're away. Away isn't like here," and he went on to complain about the Tourist Board's waste of money on advertising when the bulk of people who come for holidays to the country were Irish people who'd come anyhow, as I walked with him on the concrete, his hand on my shoulder, the tongue of the bell in my hand, the small bodies milling about us; but in three days I had his letter of permission and by the end of the month I was in London.

"Read whatever you want as long as you don't make noise," I say to placate the growing restlessness of the class in the day and they rush to take out comics. I'll make no more pretence at teaching this day. The end that I foresaw that day we went to Howth will come formally tonight at eight. I am almost glad. The long burden of deception and concealment will be over.

I found a teaching job in East London and once I got used to the Cockney speech it was little different from working in the Dublin school. I'd be back there in a year. I might as well do something different now that I had the chance. I gave up the school and worked as a clerk in an army surplus warehouse for some weeks before finding a job as barman in a small South Kensington pub.

The thronged vastness of London was the natural element of my need to be alone and slowly I was seeing that for the first time in my life I was free. She had given me a death instead of a love, but it had taken the sexual death to burn out the first death, and give me my life late but at last. The sexual need to share that life remained. If I was lucky I'd find someone I liked as well as loved, the dream of a friend and a beloved in one, a person as well as a body. When I thought on all the intimate and speeding hours I had spent with women and thought of spending the same time with a similar number of the men I knew I shuddered. It was all pleasure of blind instinct. Once the instinct was satisfied it was the person I'd have to live with. And except for the pleasure it gave in return for its satisfaction the instinct was as blind and brutal as birth or death. Only if I was lucky would I find what I was searching for, a friend and a beloved in one, and she would not be young.

I had unlocked the iron shutters and door and was wiping the tabletops the morning she came into the bar. She asked for coffee.

I was about to tell her we didn't serve coffee when I saw how lovely and tall she was, the long hair falling over the black leather of the coat she wore.

"We don't usually serve coffee but if I see if we have some would Instant do?"

"That's fine," she said and sat at one of the tables.

She was thumbing through a copy of *This Week in London* when I brought her the coffee. She opened a small clasp purse to pay.

"It's free," I said. "We don't serve coffee but since you're the first customer I made it."

"I wouldn't have asked if I had known," she was embarrassed.

"It's all right. In Ireland—where I come from—they serve coffee in the bars but seldom here."

"Why's that?"

"The breweries have a monopoly here. They make more money on the alcohol and soft drinks. You're American?" I asked.

She had come from New York City two days before. She had not come on holidays. Her father, who lived in London, wanted her to remain here. She was not yet sure whether she would stay or for how long.

"Have you worked here long?" she asked as I moved to leave the table, feeling I might be intruding with too many questions.

"For some weeks. I got a degree last summer and they gave me a year's leave of absence for one year from the school where I teach in Ireland. I thought I'd use the year to move round London in different jobs."

"That sounds like a marvellous idea."

"Except all jobs are much the same."

I had used her question to try to raise myself socially in her eyes above my barman's apron, as if it would change who I was in either her eyes or my own. Though in the brutal social scale I knew that nothing else counted except what you did or to what or whom you were connected, and it served this world—the only one it appears we'll ever have—better than any philosophy of the person. I looked at the clock. The pub was then twenty minutes open. In another ten minutes Jimmy, the other barman, would arrive. On the manager's days off we alternated in opening the bar. Any minute the early customers would start to straggle in.

"Would you like me to show you one or two of the pubs in the old part of the city?"

"I have to have dinner with my father this evening."

"What about some other evening?" And when she hesitated I said, "It needn't compromise you in any way. I'm a stranger in this city too."

"Okay," she answered with an embarrassed toss of the head.

"Tomorrow then?"

"Fine . . ."

The first customer had entered. Hurriedly we arranged to meet at seven outside the Adelphi in the Strand. She finished her coffee and rose, "See you tomorrow," as I went behind the bar.

"Well, what have you just been up to, Patrick?" the tweedy regular joked as I poured him his usual large Haig and soda. The barroom banter of the day had started.

I was at the theatre before seven, not very certain that she'd come; she might have simply agreed to the meeting as the easiest way out of the proposal; but she came under the theatre canopy at exactly seven, a grey rain cape loose on her shoulders and a red beret rakishly on her fair hair against the evening drizzle.

"I thought you mightn't come," I said out of relief.

"Why? I never break promises," she smiled.

"I had no way of knowing that."

Because of the rain I only took her the few hundred yards down the Strand to Henekey's. Upstairs in the wine-room we found a table at the window, where we could watch the wet gleam of the Strand under its lamps, and the traffic come and go over Waterloo Bridge.

"It's too wet to show you many places tonight," I said when I'd asked for the bottle of the house claret and some Cheddar.

"It's lovely here and anyhow it's much nicer to stay in one place."

"Have you decided yet to stay or go back?" I asked as we drank the claret.

"My father wants to buy me an apartment and I think I'll stay if only to avoid going back to the States for a while."

"If he'll buy an apartment and you don't want to go back why are you so hesitant?"

"I don't trust him," she said.

"Why?" I asked and she started to speak hesitantly about her father as we sipped the wine in the hushed murmurs of the wine-bar, dim from dark wood and shaded lamps, the roar and swish of traffic outside the windowpane.

"It's not an easy story to tell, in fact it's fairly incredible, and it's very American in spite of its European base. He lives in a big house in Holland Park. He has an English wife younger than I am, two kids, halfsisters of mine. He works—if you can call it work—as an interior decorator, but that's just a distraction, a lifelong obsession with rooms. The real money comes from an older woman who's been infatuated with him for years and whom he treats abominably. They have a flat they share in Mayfair, with servants. He has a bachelor flat in St. James's as well, and a permanent suite in the big hotel where I'm staying now. He has an office, of course, and staff, and he does do some decorating; he has in fact a sort of talent for it, but he isn't capable of work, in fact he can't keep his mind on anything for long. What he really does is shuttle back and forth between these two or three lives and eat and eat. It took me a long time to admit it but I suppose—he used the words of the old song himself—he's just a gigolo."

"The older woman must have money then?" I asked. There seemed such a direct intimacy between us as we sat and drank and I watched the play of her eyes in the halflight; and I trusted every word she said, but it was so outside my own life that it was like listening to someone describe a film they had just come from.

"Millions. Plus an enormous country house and a plantation in the Bahamas. She's seven or eight years older than my father. She has a grown son and daughter who hate him of course. The husband's dead. He was much older than she was. Shipping and textiles and several other things make up the fortune."

"Does he sleep with her then?" It sounded even more now like a film, *Corruption in High Society*.

"I guess so. That must be part of the bargain."

"Have you been to this big country house?"

We'd finished the basket of Cheddar and biscuits. I ordered a second bottle of the wine. Her eyes were brilliant and her talk excited.

"No. He's tried several times to get me to go but even though I've been curious to see it I've never gone. He's always trying to involve me as deeply as himself in the business but I've kept as well clear of it as possible."

"Do the two households know of one another?" I asked, my initial incredulity overcome by curiosity and fascination.

"They do but they pretend not to. It's gotten into the gossip columns. Once Caroline was tipsy and said, 'I suppose you're away to that bloody wife of yours now.' I suppose the poor woman was made to pay in one way or another for that indiscretion; my father rides roughshod over all convention, obviously. For instance, they all went skiing together. My father and Caroline travelled first class, the wife and kids, second; and they stayed in opposite wings of the same hotel at St. Moritz."

"That's too much," I said.

"I know, but I told you it was fairly incredible. But you, you've told me nothing about your life, while I've talked too much about mine. I'm not used to so much wine."

"Compared to that there's very little to tell," I grimaced ruefully and said, "Where'll I begin?"

"Your parents," she said, and I started to tell quickly.

Last Orders had been called and the darksuited waiter was clearing the tables of empty glasses and bottles. We were both tipsy.

"Since you're staying in London would you like me to take you to a game on Saturday?" I asked as I had asked my first love if she'd come to the Dress Dance at the year's end.

"That would be great fun," she said and we arranged to meet beside the ticket machines of a station close to the ground.

"Would you like to come back with me to the hotel to see the suite there?" she asked tentatively as we left.

"I'd love it," I said, though the directness of what I imagined to be a sexual invitation took my breath away.

The rain had stopped and we walked through the latenight streets to the hotel. Its bars and restaurants were closed, the night porters on and a man sat in silence behind the lighted reception desk. I followed her across the carpet of the silent lobby and marvelled at the assurance with which she said, "Fourteen, please," to the elevator man. The man said, "Thank you," on the fourteenth floor and we walked down a short corridor to the suite. On either side of the entrance hall were two large rooms with their bathrooms, two beds, armchairs, TV set, and fridge.

"This is the room my father uses," she said entering the room on the right, and I went even more silent as she opened the fridge. It displayed two bottles of champagne. "My father always keeps champagne in the fridge. Probably it's as much for ostentation as to liquor up whatever ladies come his way," she said as she closed the door.

We crossed into the room she used, where she hung her raincape in the closet and opened the liquor cabinet. She asked me if I'd like a brandy. "I think I've had enough," I refused. "I've had too much," she said and sat on one of the beds. "What do you think of it?" she asked as I came towards her from the windows that looked for miles over the night city.

"I think it costs a lot of money."

"It does. I thought it would be fun for you to see."

It was then I tried to take her in my arms. She pushed me firmly back and the tone of her, "No," left no doubt but that she meant what she said.

"See you on Saturday, I hope," she said as I left. I would

not have kept the meeting if she had not brought it up. I repeated the name of the Underground station and the time and left.

I felt she'd made a fool of me taking me to the hotel bedroom as I went down with the silent liftman and crossed the empty lobby; the world of the evening, of her long and beautiful body that I could not touch already half imaginary. I would meet her on the Saturday and take her to the game and when it was over I would bid her goodbye.

She was waiting at the row of ticket machines when I came out of the station. She had on the same black leather coat as the morning she came into the pub and she was laughing. One of the machines was automatically hiccoughing all its tickets out on the ground, two Asian collectors frantically gathering this sudden confetti.

"Someone put in a coin and it just went crazy," she explained. We stood about in a crowd that had gathered to watch the machine pump itself empty. Everybody was in good humour except the two collectors by the time the machine had emptied its load of tickets out on the ground and had gone stolidly silent again. "Everybody gets a kick out of seeing a machine turn human," I said as we moved away. Outside the station the day was shining and she said she could eat something when I asked if she was hungry. We went into a pub called the Pig and Whistle between the station and the ground. She had a bottle of cider with her sandwich and I drank bitter. She insisted on paying as she said I had paid for the wine of the previous evening but there was no other reference to the evening. I was cold and politely separate, intent on seeing her completely out of my life as soon as the game was over.

"Are you fond of ball games?" she asked as we watched the play from the terraces.

"Not as much I used to be."

I did not tell her I had almost a passion for it once: the winter nights I had watched, the floodlights on, rain drizzling into the light like spun sugar, across the lighted pitch single cigarette points glowing red and fading in the dark, and all around you the dark roaring of the crowd as the play ebbed and flowed about the big white ball in the light. I had often come all the way from Dublin to London on match excursions.

"And you, what do you notice or like about it?"

"The enormous thighs of the players," she laughed.

"They've been developed for this one purpose since they were children," I laughed with her on the terrace in the sun and when I heard her laugh, and noticed how tall and lovely she was, and thought if it was different the good times we could possibly have together, but as intent as ever of walking out of her life as soon as the game was over, when suddenly a goal was scored and as the fierce roar of the crowd went up she gripped my hand.

That sudden handclasp threw me again into confusion: perhaps, perhaps after all, it was still possible. When the teams went off at the interval we sat on coats under the metal barrier and watched police dogs leap through blazing hoops in the centre of the pitch. Each successful leap got a polite, slavish round of applause. The players came on the field again as the police took their dogs and equipment away. Play had just restarted when she turned and told me she was bored.

"We'll leave then," I said.

"But I don't mind staying."

"It's a dull game anyhow. We'll go."

We pushed our way up the terraces and went down under the stands. Outside the gate a mounted policeman kept bored watch on the empty Victorian street. After the noise of the stadium the little streets were very silent. "Are you doing anything this evening?" I asked cautiously and waited. "Nothing," the answer I hoped for came. "Maybe we could go to the park then and eat something later."

We caught a bus to a local park and walked there, under the trees that wore their first shading of green. We stood and watched the band play and a little way off a father was bowling to his child, their wicket a jacket thrown over the handle of a luncheon basket. The fallow deer nosed their nettingwire for the lettuce leaves the children brought, "Too delicate and beautiful to live free," I said; and on the artificial lake boys rowed boisterously for their girls, "It's an awful age," she said. "In all that noise just listen to their fear." Red metal tables were arranged outside a pub on the edge of the park. She sat at one while I took drinks out from the counter. Most of the couples at the other tables were parents restoring themselves at the end of the holiday, while they kept watch on their children riding the coinslot rocking-horse with the flaring scarlet nostrils or sliding down the metal shoot into the sand pit in the pub playground beyond the tables.

"Do you think a man and woman can talk as friends, without sex necessarily coming into it?" she asked suddenly.

"I don't see why not," I answered slowly. "Isn't it a person we talk to while we sleep with bodies. Though of course to have both in one is the old ideal but it doesn't happen often. Why do you ask?" Both of us had the quiet of people who expect nothing. Whatever came of the day, if it came, would come as a gift and not as any right.

"No particular reason, but I was remembering a politician I used to know in New York. He said: 'Bed first, talk later'."

"What did you say?"

"I said, 'No'."

"And he?"

"He said: 'No bed, no talk. If you change your mind here's my number.' What do you think of that?"

"I think it's usual. If you said yes he'd have got what he wanted—sex without having to waste time getting to know the person. I remember reading somewhere how Lloyd George had some Polish countess in bed before they discovered they hadn't a word of one another's language or any common language."

"That must have been funny; no doubt it was gotten over somehow. Do you think there is always some form of sexuality between the sexes?"

"I suppose so. Which brings you back to the usual brutality of the activity and the old dream of the lover and friend in one," I was uncomfortable in the conversation; it touched too close to being a garbled version of part of my own mind.

"But that hardly ever seems to happen in life."

"Isn't anything difficult always rare?" I was impatient.

"That's for sure."

"And you, have you slept with many men?"

"I've slept with men. With one exception, always someone I was emotionally interested in. And you?"

"Yes. I've slept with women."

"But did you ever find that ideal relationship?"

"I suppose I'd be married, wouldn't I, if I had."

It had grown cold at the tables. The other couples had gone and the children had been collected from the playground where the coinslot rocking-horse stood still. "It's a bit too early to eat. Why don't we have a drink inside and then go to eat?" And she agreed. The small billiard table was empty and I got a coin from the barman and we started to play. We were both equally bad, knocking almost all of the red mushrooms, and when the balls stopped coming back we put the cues in their racks and finished the drinks at the counter. We got a bus that went through the park to a small Chinese restaurant I knew close to the river. We shared a big bowl of clear soup, slices of liver and turnip and mushrooms with vegetables whose names I didn't know in the soup, delicate blue flowers engraved on the bowl. "Chinese food is so clean," she said. "I only got to know it since I came to London," I had to admit. She had chicken and almonds next, and I asked for a steamed fish. I marvelled at how easily she used the chopsticks.

"It's nothing. My father was a stickler for such nonsenses, but what does it matter? It's the same food."

"It's still nice to be able," I argued.

"I suppose so but I hate the mystique people surround such things with, doing everything the 'correct' way; and the miseries I've seen people suffer, when it's mostly a lot of baloney."

She had told me on the bus she'd been married for five

years but had left the marriage six years ago. We were both the same age. I asked her as she ate if she had anybody now in her life. She paused and I noticed how beautiful her long fingers were about the slips of wood as she looked at me directly and said, "No." There was an affair that ended two months ago: "The man was the same age as my father, a playing out of an old obsession. It is the only relationship I've ever regretted, it was sordid in some way."

"Would you have married this man?"

"Maybe eventually, but he was married; and between his concern for me and his ailing wife it was all back-and-forth stuff. He was the editor of a magazine I worked at for a time. What I find sordid was a giving up on my part, a feeling that I'd never make a life of my own, and I have to admit it was the old tune of returning to dear old daddy."

"Were you upset when it ended?"

"Well, it forced me to do some painful thinking. I ended it. He couldn't make up his mind; his wife, he said, had become an alcoholic, I had restored him, given him back his youth, and I felt only relief when it ended, but of course I was a certain age, I hadn't a relationship. I hadn't even a career."

"And your father, when it ended?"

"He was delighted. He moved in at once."

"And you've come to London."

"Yes. I never trusted the offer altogether and it was a way of getting out of New York. You can't imagine what a relief that was."

"I can well imagine," I was able to say, and I told her how I had come to London for much the same reason. As we left she said, "That was a lovely day. Thank you."

"It's a pity we can't have several such days," I said, without any hope. Since the handclasp on the terraces the day had seemed a drawn out and even somewhat beautiful farewell. She went very still and looked me still in the eyes. I reached towards her and this time she came into my arms and our lips met.

"Maybe we can have several such days after all," I said as

we parted, it was as if the farewell had been postponed, and might continue to be said over the years of our lives.

"I hope so," she said simply.

"Will you be able to spend the night with me?"

"If you want me to."

"I don't care whether we have sex or not, only to be with you and for the day to go on."

"It doesn't work that way," her voice had the quiet ring of experience.

"Will we go to the hotel or would you like to come to my place?"

"I'd like to go to your place if that's all right."

"It's all right except it's only one room."

"We'll go there. I'd like to see your room."

She said she was surprised how clean the small room was, and I told her I only used it to sleep or read in but the books made it tolerable. "Do you have any cooking facilities?" she asked. I told her there was a gas cooker I was supposed to share with a young couple who had a child next to the bathroom, but I hardly ever used it. The husband was a policeman.

"It's not much after that suite you showed me at the hotel."

"I prefer it here. It's your room. The hotel is public."

I watched her drape her clothes on the back of the chair in the halflight and she came quickly and completely naked into my arms. In a wonder my hands went over and over her beautiful woman's body and as soon as I moved closer she opened to me.

"Why didn't you let me in the hotel room?" I asked afterwards.

"I couldn't. I didn't know you. And I didn't want to enter any relationship so soon after the last one I told you about. And I could see your amazement at the hotel suite over the whole story of my father. It was too funny, in a way; your eyes were practically coming out of your head when I told you about the skiing holiday. We were so strange to one another. It wouldn't have been right."

"You've slept with no one since that last business?" I

couldn't help asking, though I hated and feared my already growing possessiveness.

"No one."

"But why did you ask me back to the hotel room?"

"I thought it would be fun for you to see. I wanted to draw out the evening. I was attracted to you, it was a way of breaking down the strangeness. I guess I hoped we'd meet again."

"But what did you expect me to think?"

"It was stupid of me, and I'm not used to so much wine. What did you think?"

"I thought you were fooling with me."

"You don't have to think that anymore," her lips searched for mine, and all night we lay awake in one another's arms as if the day was continuing. About four the policeman's child started to cry and we heard the door open on the landing and someone lighting the gas stove. The door closed again. Soon the child stopped crying. Day was beginning to come into the small room. She asked me if I knew the policeman or his wife and I told her, "Only to pass on the stairs, but once she borrowed sugar. There seemed no point getting to know people in a big city. They might turn out very boring and then you'd be stuck or have to change rooms. And anyhow I wanted to be alone."

When we rose she offered to make coffee on the stove outside but we both agreed it'd be nicer to go out. "We can go to the hotel if you want. It would cost nothing." "Who pays for it then?" "Caroline eventually, it goes through a travel agent." "We'll go there if you want, but some neutral place might be nicer," I said. She too preferred a neutral place.

We found a café open near Liverpool Street Station: it was ajostle with crowds from the Sunday market, many of them Jews. We had bacon and eggs on toast and white coffee.

"It's like an American breakfast. Except the coffee is better in the States," she said, and began to tell me her life. I finger her words like worn coins as I remember her voice in the little café. I try to animate them by turning them into my own life, I garland them with memory, embellish them with what

I know, and remember in some dismay that we can only love what we know.

A child is riding on a bus from her school in the Berkshires into New York. Her father is waiting for her at the terminal with tickets for a concert he has promised to take her to for her birthday. His eyes light on her gloveless hands as she gets off the bus and he is furious she is not wearing one of the pairs of white gloves he gave her for the birthday and he returns her to the school on the next bus back to the Berkshires. And that bus will be forever in my mind a green bus moving between the whitethorns of Ireland, the father at the terminal the greying madman I was to meet twenty years later, and the child riding back to the Berkshires is not my beloved when she was young but some sister on a day a waxen head of a doll had shattered. I watched my own words too pass behind the mask of the lovely face across the table; and if that seachange happens to your coinage, my love, what may become of mine? We will pay and leave and walk instead in the day among the stalls of the market.

"I guess I better start thinking of getting back to the hotel," she said when we reached the head of the market. The weak sunlight spun gold in her hair, gleaming on the brown hornclasp.

"Why?"

"Pop is bound to be jumping up and down over something or other."

"When will we meet again?" I asked and we arranged to meet the next day but first I'd ring the hotel in case there were complications with the father.

"And you, love, what will you do for the rest of the day?"

"I don't mind being alone. And I think I'll ring Jimmy at the bar and go on for the night. He likes to get Sunday nights off."

"So much has happened in the last twenty-four hours that I feel I need to be alone in order to catch up. It's funny how that kind of catching up has always got to be done alone," she more thought aloud than spoke as we lingered over the parting.

"How can I be sure you won't just disappear out of my life?"

"You'll have to trust me," she smiled. "But here, take this," she slipped a lapis lazuli in a wide silver band from her finger and handed it to me. "Keep it for me till tomorrow."

The rest of that day was the very best of my life, the most that life can give. A charm wreathed itself around everything. As I retraced our walk by Liverpool Street Station I dropped a note in the beggar's cap who was sitting between his crutches near the news-stand and did not wait for his reaction. At the dustbin outside Dirty Dick's I paused and felt if I emptied my pockets—money and biro and diary and watch—into it I'd walk the more lightly and free, and then said, "You eejit," to the whim and passed on. The very consciousness that the charm I saw in everything did not belong to the things or people themselves, but that I was making them up, and that they'd disappear with a simple change of feeling, only made these links of sensation in the hours' chain of ecstasy more precious still. When I tired of walking I rang Jimmy and offered to relieve him at the bar for the evening session. He said he didn't mind working as he owed me weekends, but he was still only too eager for the Sunday night off.

Mr. Plowman, the manager, and I were the only two on. We were fairly busy in the early part of the evening, but towards closing time it tailed off. It was always the same on Sunday night unless a strange party came in but no strangers appeared that night. We had covered the pump handles and I was wiping the tables waiting for the last few customers to leave before locking up when she appeared in the doorway with a small travelling bag. I was so amazed that Plowman had already said, "Sorry, madam. We're closed," before I spoke. "It's all right. She's a friend," I explained and introduced them. "Won't you please take a seat?" he offered with his usual courtly gesture of the hand. "Patrick won't be long." "Would you like something to drink while we're washing up?" I asked but she shook her head and said she was all right. She'd sit and read. I was never as grateful for Plowman's decent English reserve: "I know exactly what I'm doing, and

I trust you know the same about what you're doing, and what we do is our own business as long as we pay our bills," while she read and he counted the takings and locked them in the safe in the office and I went through the last of the chores. When we finished he asked, "Would your friend like to join us for our nightcap?" and I relayed awkwardly, "The manager is inviting you to join us for a drink."

"Patrick and I always have a drink at the end of the day," he said jocularly, pouring himself a large Scotch, and taking a fresh cigar from the tin after offering it round. I had a beer and we chatted for about twenty minutes on those genial coinages that make no demands and cause no tensions, but tonight they hung heavy as lead in the cigar smoke, so fierce was the desire to be alone with her, to discover why she had come or what had happened back at the hotel, and she was the first to speak when we left, the side door of the bar clicking behind us. "Can I stay with you tonight?" she turned to me tensely. "Of course. I'm delighted you came but I got a shock when you came in, that was all. Surely it goes without asking that you can stay and for as long as you wish," there was some of the tense gravity of a child asking a favour and I was tempted to tease her.

"I wasn't sure," she drew away.

"The day didn't go so well then?"

"It was awful. There were loads of messages at the hotel, all from my father. He had arranged dinner for me with this lawyer he's been trying to pimp me off on for years, and then you couldn't be found, he shouted. He'd bought me this flat. He was setting me up, backing me to the hilt, and I wasn't contributing. Just sitting on my fat ass, were the words. I was irresponsible and crazy and I hated him, that was the line. And then, when he drove me back to the hotel, he turned to me in a pale fury and said, 'You're just like a dead bird round my neck.' I went into the hotel and took this bag and left." Her voice was breaking.

"Don't worry. You can stay as long as you like if the old room's all right."

"It's marvellous," she said. "Anywhere to be away from all that and to be with you," she drew me towards her.

"And did you see this flat?"

"Yes. It's in South Kensington, very close to here. It's rather grand. And he's having a ball doing it up. It's full of workmen. It's his new toy."

The days that followed passed in dangerous happiness, so much so that the thought as I hurried home—for the room had become a home—was that I would find her gone. When I opened the door I felt touched by the same panic as the idea that one day I'd have to die caused whenever it stole without warning into my mind, but always she was in the room, the small table laid, and she'd light the candle in its centre before switching off the electric light, and by the candleflame we'd eat and talk before falling into one another's arms, the happiest moment of the lovemaking the sharp little cry or catch of the breath she gave when she came, and lingeringly we'd kiss before turning away into our own sleep. On days off from the pub we'd walk in the mornings through the street markets buying green pepper and parsley and eggs and meat and bread and butter. I'd go for a bottle of cheap claret while she left the door open to cook our lunch on the stove on the landing; and after we'd eaten, drowsy with the wine, we'd draw the curtain and fall into the bed, rising when people were leaving their offices and we'd walk the evening together through the ever varying streets of London.

"Sometimes I'm afraid it's a dream," she used say. "It's incredible that two people should feel so easy together."

A Sunday came, a Sunday I had off from the bar, a hot London Sunday. We had coffee and eggs and toast in the same little café close to Liverpool Street and afterwards as we walked in the sun through the stalls and throngs of the market she suddenly said, "Why don't we go to the hotel for lunch? It won't cost us anything." "How will you manage that?" I asked. "I'll just sign the bill with the suite number." "Won't it be checked?" I was apprehensive. "Of course not. It goes through the account. Compared to what's spent, a lunch is a drop in the bucket." "Aren't you afraid of meeting your father?" I felt cloddish with all the questions. "What if we do? But we won't. Sunday is his familyman day. Come on, let's go." "All right, let's go," I fell into her mood. We walked through the empty city, a few tourists on the steps of St. Paul's, and up a silent Fleet Street into the broad Strand. As it was drawing close to one o'clock we took a bus from Charing Cross which dropped us a few yards from the hotel.

The restaurant was a great babbling cavern after the sunlight of the street. A headwaiter in formal black ticked a table off on a typed list and a little Spanish waiter in a red-tailed vest over black pants showed us to the table in broken English.

"Will you have anything to drink?" he asked. "We'll wait a little," I replied.

"It's fun here on Sundays," she said. "I love full restaurants. I knew a couple in New York who went broke running a restaurant. It was awful watching them drink at the bar among all the empty tables, seeing the whole place go slowly broke. So many dreams are put into a restaurant. When you see one empty it's like watching dreams go slowly broke."

"This place certainly shows no sign of going broke," I looked around at the crowded restaurant. Behind a copper counter white-hatted chefs raced about in the kitchen. Outside the counter a whole side of beef rested on a butcher's table, kept heated by infra-red lights in the corners of the ceiling above the copper. "I always feel in a place like this someone is going to come up to me and tap me on the shoulder and say We've checked up on you. You shouldn't be here, you must leave."

"Well, then, you just leave," she started to laugh.

"But the humiliation," I groaned, and she laughed even more. "I know it makes no sense but it must be some old race instinct."

"In the States it's the opposite. Someone with self-confidence can do practically anything. It's almost as if people are anxious to take you for what you believe yourself to be. And if you're found out you simply say, what the hell.

For instance my mother left town with someone after she broke with my father and I've never laid eyes on her since. America's such a vast country that there's the feeling that if things don't work out you can get out of town. Why don't you let me order for you today?"

"Right," I was relieved, looking around at a bedlam of festivity.

"We'll start off with a Margharita. It's delicious on a hot day."

We both felt easier with the cold frosted salt of the rim of the glass and the glow of the tequila going down in the cold of the fruit juices. She asked for shrimp in the half of avocado, and two rare ribs from the side of bullock on the butcher's slab, which came with a baked potato in a silver paper and jugs of sour cream and horseradish. We had a blue cheese with the last of the red wine and finished with black coffee and Armagnac.

"I have a feeling you know so much more about life than me," I spoke out of my unease in such showy opulence.

"That's your imagination. Like the chopsticks in the Chinese place. Most women have more confidence when young than men. It's based on an idea of sexuality which doesn't serve them all that well as the years go by," she said quietly and then laughed lowly. "I never went to college though, which you did.

"My father married me off before I had a chance. Why? It was before Caroline. In time the boy would come into a lot of money, a fortune; and I suppose my father thought that through the marriage he'd have access to that money in some way. The boy's family was dead set against it but my father railroaded it through. The boy was dull and I never loved him but he was very decent and in the long run got badly hurt. For me it was the best thing that could have happened then, it got me away from my father, and I've never regretted the marriage since, except that Jason—that was his name—had to get such a raw deal."

"How, raw?"

"He was in love with me and I left him. But during those five years I was married to him I was able to rest and read and grow in the safety of that dull marriage as I'd never have been able to do with my father around.

"My father always used me. He played the concerned father worried about his difficult motherless daughter, and the ladies lapped that up, not that he wasn't attractive to women anyhow, he was; and one of those women, who became a sort of stepmother, worked herself to the bone to put me through an expensive progressive school while my father freewheeled around New York. He was still 'studying'. He was a 'genius' who hadn't yet been recognized, which was a cover-up for just doing nothing. Then he turned the headmaster into a father figure and got himself into the school by giving classes in colour design, and in my final high school year he seduced my best friend. He tried to get us to dress up in identical clothes, governess-type clothes and he sailed with the two of us off to Europe. He used to get great moon-eyes at the very mention of Europe. 'What I love about Europe', he used to say, 'is the feel of old worn stones everywhere, stones rounded by centuries of use.' Of course I didn't know she was my father's mistress when we sailed—it still amazes me how slow I was in everything that concerned him—I only found out when we were in Europe. I was hypnotized by him then."

"What did you live on in Europe?" I asked between anger at the unfairness and pure amazement.

"The usual: the girl's allowance. Most of the girls at those schools were rich, and he had rent from an apartment, and an aunt gave him the odd hundred dollars. He was still 'studying'. Everybody should contribute, be of use, he liked to say, and the funny thing is I think he still believes that when he says it, though the whole of his life has been one long suck on the tit of society.

"The girl began to make trouble, the schoolfriend. Her family had started to move in. It was then he decided to pawn me off on this boy whose family he had known for ages. He was always around money. When he'd fixed it up, he got me to write a letter to my grandfather asking if he'd house me for those six months before. I had to rewrite that letter twenty times, with him standing over me like a dancing master yelling, 'Not that, sweetie, not this, sweetie, are you stupid or what?' but anyhow my grandfather refused and the boy's family wound up paying for board and nuptials. The three of us, I remember, were travelling in the train in Italy just before the wedding and the boy said something typically American, 'Stick with me and you'll be farting through silk;' and it might give you a look into my father's mind that a year after we married he sent me beautiful white silk underwear, incredibly fine seaming with white silk thread, handstitched by the nuns in Ravenna.

"We did an idea of the Grand Tour, my father's idea, down to the dreaming spires and to punting on the Cam during the excuse of a courtship. My head was full at the time of a dream I had. I dreamt my mother was on a bier, a slab of wood, dead in her wedding dress, covered with masses of flowers, while Chopin's Funeral March was being played, one of my father's favourite pieces of music. There was a wounded silence when I came out with it, it was while we were on the Cam and when he got the punt to the bank he hustled me aside and hissed, 'Sweetie, you just don't *say* things like that to people. It's incredibly *gauche*.'

"Jason's parents tried to stop the wedding, but they were no match for my father, and they wound up picking up the check for an enormous reception at the Ritz. Afterwards my father fell into real depression, and before Jason and I flew back to the States he took us to a nightclub. He made a sick play for a singer who would have nothing to do with him. I'll never forget the gloom of that table with the champagne and roses and his favourite gardenias, and I felt it was I who had rejected him and not the singer."

The restaurant had nearly emptied when she asked for a second coffee and the check. I looked at the bill and whistled before I handed it to her across the table. She laughed as she noticed with what apprehension I watched her write *plus twelve percent* and the room number and initials and return it to the waiter. "You see, it's simple," she smiled and pulled her cardigan over the white blouse. I rose with her, saying as I watched the small waiter check the initials with the headwaiter over where the greatly diminished sides of beef stood on the slabs beside the copper counter, "I'll believe it's simple when we're out on the street," which caused her to laugh more. As they noticed us leave, the headwaiter simply nodded his approval to the waiter, who hurried towards us to bow us obsequiously out the door. "I still don't believe it. There must be some snag," I pressed her again on the street, the sunlight from glass harsh after the opulent cavern of the room. "There's none. I've seen some of the checks and there's often as much as four thousand pounds spent in a month. The day is so hot and lovely, it'd be nice if we could get out of the city," I saw the simple glass beads glitter on the long throat inside the V of the white blouse as she spoke.

"Two buses from here will take us to the forest."

"Let's go then," she put her arm eagerly in mine and we kissed before we crossed the street; and flushed with the wine we started to kiss again at the deserted bus stop, waiting for the bus to come in.

"My father was very present too at the ending of the marriage. There were more and more quarrels with Jason, mostly because I couldn't bear making love with him. I'd flinch when he'd touch me, but as I was preparing to leave him he got me pregnant.

"I was interested in having the child though hardly more than a child myself; but Jason was worried, he hadn't finished college, we were dependent on an allowance from his family. It would be a real tie. It was all tailor-made for my father to move in, and he did. It was decided I wasn't mature enough to have a child.

"Jason stayed in the States and I went with my father to Switzerland where he stagemanaged the abortion even more thoroughly than the marriage. He moved with me into the clinic, into the same room, where, as I was convalescing from the abortion, he was having a series of Bogomolitz injections, extracts from calf embryo's organs—liver and testicles—which were supposed to give him a fillip."

"But surely he couldn't move into the same room as a young woman having an abortion, even if she was his daughter?" The story disturbed and depressed me.

"With my father the unusual is the ordinary. Caroline's money was available by then. It was a private clinic. He was stagemanaging the operation. And if you are prepared to pay you can probably have any arrangement you want. One thing I remember vividly that he said before we left the clinic: 'When I'm old, sweetie, you'll be pushing me round in a wheelchair, looking out on the snow of those goddamned Swiss mountains.'

"There was no guilt at all after the abortion, I felt marvellous, as if I was clean again. I saw Jason in New York and told him I was leaving. He promised we'd make a new life, we'd have children and all that, but I'd made up my mind.

"If I'd been smart, after leaving Jason I'd have lived for a time alone but it didn't happen that way. Almost at once I was swept off my feet. I lived with him for four years. Roberto was his name. Roberto Leonelli."

"Who was he?"

"An unsuccessful writer and looking back on it a lot of other things too. He was very handsome and though I didn't know it at the time was having affairs left, right and centre all around New York while he was living with me, though I was the only one unaware of it. He was in the same mould as my father. The genius who was still studying. He wrote a novel that collected nineteen rejection slips before we got tired of sending it around. When the rejection slips would come he'd get depressed and start drinking and try to beat me up. As with my father, everything was a conspiracy against him."

"What did he make a living on?" I felt like an old record with every thread but this one line worn away.

"Often he made a lot of money, in advertising and public

relations. He had real charm. When he was writing the book, I kept him by working at odd jobs. Once when I was out of work I stole an expensive art book that I resold but I was caught and let off with a warning. Roberto was just amused when I told him. He got me to go over it in detail and put it in the book. He and my father hated one another, and my father tried every trick to break the affair up. I remember Roberto crying out after one visit, 'Will that goddamned monster *ever* leave us in peace;' he wasn't near as tough or as crazy as my father, who had the upper hand. And soon afterwards my father moved in with the offer of analysis—he had practically a free hand then with Caroline's money; he thought it might finish off the relationship, and he was right, though not in the way he expected."

"What attracted you to analysis?" I felt one more line added to the old record, numbed by the difference of the life to mine.

"I'd started to read Freud. I knew there was something wrong with me. I was constantly dropping things. One moment I'd feel all-powerful and the next that I couldn't even say hello to someone. For their different reasons both my father and Roberto encouraged me, Roberto because he'd started to feel that all his troubles were due to my frigidity, and if that could be changed all would be well again. So I jumped at the chance. I would use the analysis as a tool and try to break out of my breakdown. Looking back on it, all my life had been a walk along ledges. Nothing had ever been built up.

"For the first three of four sessions I talked nonstop, mostly around one incident. When I was eight I was living with my father outside New York City and one night when I was asleep he came into my bed and masturbated against me. When I woke up and found him there I pretended to be still asleep but in the morning I confronted him and he denied it. Once he said something in those days that was that. I know now that if I hadn't been certain he was lying at that single moment I would never have gotten free, not through analysis or anything else either. After those first three or four sessions I felt

I had described my whole life, and nothing had happened.

"Then after that I just lay on the couch and was silent, the sessions were fifty minutes long, awfully long those fifty minutes seemed. They were always the same. The doctor would smile and bow when I'd come and then he'd rise from his chair behind me to indicate the session was up and smile and bow, not a word having been uttered. I guess that's why they prefer you to pay, fifty a session, a dollar a minute of silence, you *better* say something . . .

"The first breakthrough happened around the relationship with Roberto, and it was painful to admit that everything wasn't what I wanted to think it was, that there were fights and lies and much squalor. I felt I was betraying him by admitting that. In order to articulate those vague doubts and resentments floating around in my mind I had to break down all the defences against articulating them—that was what was painful—and to do that I had to relive them again in order to see through to what caused the defence to be put up in the first place; painful too because the defence had been originally put up as a block against the pain of seeing that my life was not as I wanted or imagined it to be. As the relationship with Roberto was a living or acting out of what I had felt for my father, it was weak enough to come first to the surface. The stone falling in the water throws out circles, it was the outer circle, the beginning of the journey from circle to inner circle, down to the stone in the mud of the river.

"No, the doctor said nothing throughout the journey, he just sat there and sometimes he'd say 'Can you go on?' or 'That's interesting' or at the most 'That was well done,' which was important in this way: I remember well going to my father for praise when I was four or five, having succeeded in tying my shoelaces for the first time, and his only reaction was to glower indifference, when if *he'd* said 'That was well done' it would have given the confidence that I was loved, without which it seems impossible to grow normally. Though the inward reliving of the life and seeing why and how the defences and blocks came into being was really a perverse way of acquiring a natural upbringing, it was as much a substitute for it as an artificial limb is for a lost limb, but without that artificial limb I would never have been able to walk into my own life. Sometimes as I travelled from circle to inner circle it grew so painful that I got up from the couch and faced the doctor. That was useless. The painful going inwards was replaced at once by social surfaces, the surfaces of watching his reactions, and gently he'd persuade me to lie down on the couch again, where I'd be forced to be alone. Sometimes too the very power of the recollected emotion, as when I recalled my grandfather's house, the only constant house throughout my childhood, it's tall white columns, the long avenue of elms, fir trees on either side of the house where lights hung at Christmas, I'd break down in tears, and the doctor would still sit there in silence behind me, waiting for me to go on."

"And did you come to the stone in the mud?"

"Yes, circle by slow circle, so hard to see simply because it had all the time been under my nose. My father, having denied or crushed every attempt I made as a child to reach towards a life with his love, once he noticed me come into my own sexual life he started to woo—in that way he's like a tone-deaf music lover: the only value he sees in anything is when he sees others value it. In seduction he's very clever, as by the way was Roberto. They're both totally passive; and having no instinct of their own to rely on they have to depend on their ability to read or play on what others desire, they become mirrors in which each person may read what they will, and they seduce by being seduced. All Don Juans fit into that pattern. What he played most on was my desire for loyalty, and since I'd gotten none as a child the desire for it was fierce. So the early hatred was replaced by an 'in-loveness', a confusion of loathing and adoration.

"I was in love then with my father and since it was a shameful love it came out in the form of guilt. The suffering was in working past this taboo. I felt the breaking of the taboo was a betrayal of Roberto, which was just another form of the earlier guilt."

"What did you feel then when you found the stone in the mud of the river?"

"That for the first time my life was at zero. I had my artificial limb and a life. It was up to me. I owe so much to that doctor . . ."

"Then you left this Roberto?"

"Not immediately. He had always been threatening to leave, which had played on the old anxiety of being abandoned, but the last time he threatened I said, 'Okay;' and helped him pack and called a cab. No, he did nothing, I don't think he believed it. And when the door shut and I was alone, the silence around me was stunning.

"It's strange how there seems to be some need for a ritual end. I discovered a rat in the apartment some weeks after Roberto left. I called the rat exterminator. One night I came home to find it dying in the sink. I put on a pair of rubber gloves and lifted it by the tail and dropped it down the rubbish chute, I felt that was *really* the end. The curtain was drawn, the audience had gone, and the ushers were coughing and waiting for me to leave."

She laughed, a clear bright-eyed laugh. When the bus did come we paid the conductor on our way up the stairs to the empty top deck. We went up to the very front left-hand seat. Even when we'd screwed all the front windows wide open it was still very hot.

"Why is it so empty?" she asked.

"Some of these routes are often very empty on Sunday. It's probably the last run of their shift for the crew, and they're probably ahead of their schedule, which is why it's crawling so."

"It was a marvellous day," she kissed me on the throat. I put my hand over her neck to globe the rich breast in the blouse but then bold with desire draped the raincoat over our thighs and under it slipped my free hand through the fold in the wraparound corduroy skirt. My hand was free to fold and stroke into her sex under the coat.

"It's very bold," she said.

"What does it matter?"

We played with our desire as the bus limped through Holborn and the empty City and out through Hackney and across the green of the Leyton Marshes with its Sunday footballers in their bright strips between the many white goals and others just with jackets down and playing in their shirts and trousers. We had to wait for a change of bus at the Bakers, aflame with desire in the indolence of the hot Sunday. As soon as the bus came and had passed the first few stops into the forest, I said, "I suppose we can get off at any stop we like."

"The sooner the better," she urged and we got off at the next stop.

We hurried down a green bank and into an opening in the trees. The earth was bare and dark under the trees and smelled of dead leaves.

"Quick," she said kicking off her sandals and unknotting the cord of the skirt so that it folded away and slid to the raincoat. I wanted to delay a moment to look on the lovely white thighs on the raincoat in the middle of the dark clay but she said again, "Quick," and as I entered her she moved violently and with a cry searched for my mouth as I moved within her a last time. A small black fly on her face brought us back to where we were and she said, "There's no use pushing our luck. You never know who might come by," and she rose and quickly wrapped the skirt around her and knotted the cord and slipped her feet back in the sandals. She laughed when I said, "That didn't take long." "I should think not." And then she said gently, stroking my hair, "It was marvellous. It was a marvellous day. It never happened to me like this before." "I should hope not," I smiled and started to pick out three dead leaves that had tangled in her hair.

Afterwards we groped our way through the forest till we reached an artificial lake, on which boats were racing back and forward. We sat on an empty bench close to the boathouse, and she started to talk again as she had talked in the restaurant and at the bus stop.

"I made no mistake this time in rushing into another

relationship. Those first months I spent alone were the best time of my life till then.

"My father was delighted by the turn of events. He sent me tickets to come to Europe and he made me a present of various charge accounts. On hot days in New York, when everybody was going crazy, it was marvellous to be able to hire a car and drive out to the sea around the Hamptons. The most useful thing I learned from the freedom of the charge accounts was that indulgence was depressing. Rather like a child hurrying to a party, all expectation, and then emptiness.

"After a year I had a couple of affairs, sometimes fun and sometimes enjoyable simply for the company and sex but it wasn't what I was looking for or wanted. And then I fell in love, love in the sense of anxiety and loss, and constant longing.

"I think one of the reasons was that it was the first time I was rejected, I was used to being pursued and at first he was infatuated with me. It's a common shape: the man gets infatuated with the woman; the woman in her egotism grows infatuated with the man's infatuation; the man withdraws and the woman finds herself suffering the tortures of the dammed. I found myself hanging round the apartment like a sick cow all day, waiting for the phone to ring, escaping to movie houses, and in the movie house panicking that the phone might be ringing while I was away . . . but once I decided it was hopeless, that was that. I met him at parties afterwards and felt nothing and I began a short affair almost at once. The man was young and very rich and he pushed me very hard to go out with him soon after we met though I explained that I was recovering from a bad time. 'Never mind. We'll play it by ear,' he said and that's just what we did. He was young and sensual; we sailed weekends on his yacht and went to the Bahamas. It lasted for two months, and I enjoyed the luxury and simple ease of the sexuality. He didn't want to involve himself any more than I did: yes, it was a long sensual bath after the sufferings, a healing romp."

"Why didn't you continue the affair with him if you'd enjoyed it and had no stronger attachment?" I was curious.

"I probably would have in the same situation."

"But you're a man. For me it was over. It seems that simple sensuality can only go so far for a woman, and once that happened and it could go no further I had no more interest in the sexuality."

"Since you were immune, recovering from suffering, it could have been dangerous for him? He might have fallen in love with you."

"He wasn't capable of that kind of feeling, and anyhow it didn't turn out that way."

"And then you had the affair with the married man?"

"That's the only affair I regret. There would have been more dignity in waiting for an equal relationship, just in the waiting."

We watched youths in two boats race one another on the artificial lake and as they collided almost capsize a third. We rose from the seat to move to the road and stop. I put my arm round her waist and she clasped tight my hand as I said, "Sometimes I get jealous of those other men."

"That's silly. No more than I should be jealous of those other women. We didn't know of one another's existence then. It'd be different if it happened now."

"But I'm glad you've had those affairs, if you hadn't, with a body lovely and strong as yours, it would have been a kind of waste. I don't think it's even jealousy. It's basically a resentment at nonexistence. I can imagine those affairs but I can't imagine the world after my death, though I'll be as nonexistent to everything then as I was in your life when you knew those other men."

"What a solemn speech," mockingly she teased my hair.

A bus was coming in the far distance, "Let's run," and we caught it and with a change of bus at the Bakers we were back in the room within the hour. "Will you marry me?" I asked her as we fell on to the small bed. "Of course I will." Gently and slowly we made love, and when it was over she said, "I'm thinking that I should go back to the hotel. Would you mind if I did?"

"No, but why?"

"Just in case my father is worried. I disappeared so completely after that row. Just to check," and after she made coffee on the outside stove she left for the hotel. I was puzzled by this sudden desire to go back to the hotel after the day but I trusted her now and shrugged and went round the corner to the local for a glass of beer.

It was late when she came back to the room and she was very excited.

"Pop took me to dinner," she explained. "He can be so nice when he wants to be."

"Why should he *not* be nice?" I was tired and irritated with waiting for her to come back.

"I don't know. I'm always so relieved when things are simple and go well."

"I used to be that way. Now if someone isn't civil I don't see any reason to see them again. Just tell them to fuck off."

"Don't be angry. I'm glad I went back to the hotel. He was worried. He didn't know where I'd gone to. He'd even contacted the police, which is really something if you know him. The flat is finished. It's actually quite lovely. Caroline is ill in hospital and—hold everything—he wants to meet you."

"Did you tell him I work in a bar?"

"No. I told him you were about to finish your doctorate, which is kind of true, and it makes it socially easier."

"From all you've told me I'm not exactly dying with desire to meet him."

"It'll be useful to me if you'll meet him."

"And which of these households is the meeting to take place in?"

"In the bosom of the family. For dinner. He warned me that you must never know about Caroline and that other household. How can he imagine that I could live with you and love you and conceal things like that from you?"

"People reveal themselves in those kind of warnings. *He* probably could without bother."

"That's his whole life, but when can you make it for?"

"We might as well get it over with at once. Tomorrow?"

"He actually suggested tomorrow. He's agog to meet you. Can you get off from the bar?"

"I can shuffle almost any day with Jimmy."

"I'll call him in the morning and confirm it. It's been such a long day," she said as she slid into bed, laughing over the bus ride to the forest before we fell asleep.

We were both too nervous for speech as we walked up the wide treelined avenue to the house the next evening. She carried a bunch of blue irises she'd bought beside the station. "Here," she said in a tone that reminded me of someone going to the dentist, and opened a black gate door. An awning of glass and steel covered the path and steps that led up to the front door, which was black too, but the brass in the shape of a lion's claw was highly polished. Through the glass I looked on either side from the ironbarred windows of the basement to the three floors above it.

"It's bloody enormous," I muttered.

"It won't last long. I'll know when to break it up. He'll get bored after an hour anyhow. He reminds me of the sealion, the way he flops down once a meal is finished," she spoke nervously and quickly before she pressed the button in the wall. We waited until a voice rasped out her name over the intercom and almost at once the door was released with a harsh buzzing sound. Black and white squares of marble filled the large hallway and a phone and phonebook stood with flowers on a little table in an alcove.

"The kitchen and the dining area are downstairs," she said and at the foot of the spiral staircase in another hallway, which was carpeted, her father and stepmother received us. I noticed as I went down that there were keys in all the doors. She kissed them on both cheeks, handing the stepmother the irises, using first my Christian name and then my full name as we shook hands. He was very tall, and handsome; his height and good bones and wellcut charcoal suit concealing to some extent his gross overweight. The wife was tall and plain, and though she was no more than our age there was something about her of a woman much older.

"Well, what is everybody having to drink?" he asked and took out a large bunch of keys while his wife with, "How charming," set about arranging the irises. A maid who was bent over lettuce leaves at one end of the enormous room smiled and he stopped in his progress with the keys towards the liquor cabinet to wave a casual arm, "This is Nora. She is from Ireland too."

When he'd unlocked the cabinet he took out an unopened bottle of Paddy and held it to the light. "For the occasion," he smiled. "I'm told it's the best Irish."

"It's a good whiskey," I said as I looked out on a long lawn run to a summer house half-hidden in some shrubbery at the garden's end through the glass of the white folding doors.

"That's what my Irish friends tell me, I sometimes do some business in Dublin," he said as he poured the whiskey into four glasses, adding cubes of ice from a silver bowl, and went on to name an expensive Dublin hotel, and a member of the government, whose name I was familiar with from newspapers. "They're all crooked there of course, but it's easier to do business with them when they're that way. Anyhow, I have a sneaking liking for rogues, don't you?" he pressed me, staring from under heavy lashes. "I don't have much experience of business," I answered to escape the stare, and he began to ask me about my doctorate. This was mercifully interrupted by a governess bringing in two children in their nightclothes. They were fussed over for a few minutes, the older excitedly jumping high into my love's arms, and then the governess took them upstairs again. When they'd gone he turned to his wife, "Don't you think, sweetie, it would be nicer if I lit the fire?"

"What a good idea," she said and turned on the lights in the chandelier and drew the long curtains on the lawn while he took a big box of matches from the mantel and bent to light a prepared fire of logs in the grate. He cracked several idle matches, staring at me from under his arm. I was puzzled and embarrassed by the stare—did he think, I wondered, that his stare was hidden by his arm—and I turned away on the pretext of examining books on an open shelf. When eventually the fire caught I didn't notice.

"There's nothing so warm and friendly as the old wood fire," he rubbed his hands as he rose from the blazing pile of logs. The wife had joined the maid at the big cooker and suddenly called, "Dinner's ready," in a singsong women use with children. The maid withdrew as we took our places at the oak table. He used the same box of matches to light a red candle in the centre of its uncovered wood.

She ladled out a rough vegetable soup while he uncorked a bottle of chilled muscadet. Sole followed, cooked in white wine with oysters and mussels and prawns, shallots and mushrooms. The cold muscadet changed to claret when veal and salad followed the fish, the meal ending with cheese and fruit. I was too tense to enjoy the food, but I'd heard so much about him that I watched him eat in fascination. If I hadn't to be so wary I would have felt sorry for him. Each new wine or course he strained eagerly towards, all excited anticipation; then when it came he devoured it at once, and collapsed into the boredom of satiety. It was during one of these long pauses that I noticed him pick from his daughter's plate.

"Don't," she said sharply.

"Oh, Evatt, really," the wife half scolded.

"I like to pick," he said and lifted something else from the plate.

"Don't," she said dangerously, "or I'll leave the table."

"Oh, Evatt, really," his wife said again.

"I like to pick," he smiled a disarmingly guilty smile, but he stopped.

After the coffee he led us to a large room upstairs, covered in colourful rugs and sheepskins, unlocked another liquor cabinet and asked, "Will you have cognac or Armagnac?" While the women talked on the sofa he drew me towards the window. He had plans for opening a Dublin office. Would I be interested in managing it? I had no experience of business,

I answered, again trying to avoid the questioning. "That doesn't matter. Are you interested?" "I'll have to think about it." I said. He fixed me with the great moon-eyes at the window as if impaling me into the prison of his gaze. It was certainly comical if I had not been so amazed. "You know that I have bought and fixed up a flat for Isobel?" I nodded dumbly, my love's name strange on his lips. "I can afford it, it's my right and pleasure, and it's part of her future inheritance. Why don't both of you move in before you marry? After all, we don't live in a feudal age. We live in modern times."

I thanked him and looked in her direction. She'd risen from the sofa, ready to end the evening. On the marble of the hallway he repeated to her the offer that we should move into the flat that he'd made me upstairs, this time in an exaggeratedly emotional voice.

"Thanks, Pop. I'll call you tomorrow," she said and turned with a lightness I marvelled at to kiss her young stepmother goodnight, "Thanks for the lovely evening," and we left, breathing at last the free evening of the treelined avenue.

"How do you think it went?" I asked.

"Is there any doubt?" she answered. "Generally he's bored after an hour and my god it went to almost three hours."

"What I couldn't understand was all that staring at me while pretending to light the fire?"

"You're not with it," she started to laugh. "You weren't supposed to be aware of him staring. He was subjecting you to his devastating intuition."

I too began to laugh. "I hate drinking when tense. The bars aren't closed yet. Why don't we have a beer or something in the next bar in order to relax a bit before going home."

"That's all right with me."

In a small bar beside the station she asked me what I thought of him and I had to tell her that I knew too much about him from her before the meeting to be certain of an impression, as she would about the people in my life. All I was certain of was that I did not trust him.

"So you've no interest in his Dublin job offer?"

"Of course not, but why did he make it?"

"His instinct is to involve everybody he comes into contact with emotionally," she answered generally. "But since he has no direct contact with his own emotions it has to be in the form of jobs or flats or money. And will we accept his offer of the flat then?"

"He says its yours. We don't have anything to lose. I suppose we might as well."

"Part of my inheritance," she echoed, and as we left the bar she put her hand in mine, her voice low as if she brooded on something dark and brutal. "Thanks for agreeing to meet him. It was very useful. If you had trusted him—horrible though it sounds it's quite true—I couldn't have trusted you, and everything that is between us would be completely finished in that one flash."

She went out to call him the next morning. "He was fine, no different from last night, but I've got to go around to the hotel to pick up the keys of the flat. It looks like goodbye old room."

When she returned she had an enormous bunch of keys and she was laughing. "He wanted to send around a bloody big van for our possessions. He was quite shocked when I said a taxi would take all we had."

Steps led up to the door of the big house in Kensington where the flat was. The front door opened easily but the door of the actual flat on the top of the grey-carpeted stairs was double-locked and it took us several minutes of fumbling with the keys before it opened. "It's just like Pop not to trust anybody," she said as we entered the flat. "We better practise on those locks before we leave the flat. Or we may never get back in again once we go out." The floors were of polished wood, broken by sheepskins, and white curtains hung ghostly still in the airless heat. The furniture was new and Scandinavian and belonged more to showrooms than to living rooms. An enormous bed that could sleep four or five filled the main bedroom. "It's a real Pop's effort," she beat it with her hand. "Custom made. I am sure he'd be dearly interested in what's gone on here after a few days, which is next best to joining us," and she then went round the flat, turning on taps, throwing open cupboards and windows, looking in the fridge, which had cheese and fruit and milk and even ground coffee. "He must have sent the servants around this morning," and she unlocked with a small key from the bunch what we thought to be the liquor cabinet. "There's bottles of wine—my god, Margaux—and guess what," she began to laugh, "A bottle of Paddy. What do you think of it?"

"It's all too much for me at one go. I feel something between an intruder and an invalid."

"We can leave if you feel uncomfortable."

"Why should we leave? It's free, you own it. I'll soon get used to it, don't worry. After a while you don't see rooms. I was only trying to say exactly how I feel about it. How one feels and how one acts are two completely different things."

"I certainly have no quarrel with all this but I'm used to it though I have lived without it as well and not missed it," I loved her face when it wore the melancholy of reflection.

It was soon afterwards that the phone rang in the next room, "I bet it's Pops," she said as she went to the receiver. I heard her say, "I love it. It's absolutely marvellous. I can't tell you how grateful I am." I was embarrassed listening and closed the door. She was disturbed when she came back to the kitchen. "Pop rides again. He can't give anything with one hand without taking it back with the other. When I told him how grateful I am he snarled that he didn't want my gratitude; but he sends you his best. Why don't we go out for a walk?" We got our coats and started to laugh again as we practised on the locks before closing the door. For the first time I noticed the letters for the other flats in the building laid out neatly on a little oval table in the hallway. The evening was cold and clear and I was glad after the strangeness of the flat to be walking with her in that anonymity that only public places can bestow.

The next morning she took a cane basket that had come with

the flat and went out to shop for lunch. I stayed behind because I wanted to be alone but almost as soon as she'd gone the telephone rang. I didn't pick it up as no one I knew had the number and I was afraid it was her father. It continued to bell incessantly, at four- to six-minute intervals, and I eventually left the flat. I met her on her way back from the market.

"Everything is more expensive here," she said.

"The rents are higher. The damned phone has never stopped ringing since you left."

"Why didn't you pick it up?"

"I was afraid it might be your father and I have nothing to say to him."

"That kind of manic ringing is just his style."

We heard it ring in the empty flat as we climbed the stairs but it had stopped by the time we'd opened the door. Exactly five minutes later it rang again. I picked up the extension in the kitchen as soon as I heard her say hello.

"Where the hell have you been? I've been trying to reach you all morning," he yelled at once.

"I was out shopping for lunch," she said, very matter of fact but the tone was freezing.

"Listen, sweetie," his voice changed to woo, "I want you to go in this afternoon to see Caroline." I went very tense at the mention of the rich woman's name. "She's been very good to *us*."

"Don't mix me up in it," I heard her say suddenly in a cold fury. "She's been very good to *you*."

"Who do you think bought every stitch on your back? Who do you think bought the goddamned flat you're nesting out in?" he yelled.

"What she bought she gave because she chose to and that's totally her affair and yours. I'll go into the hospital this afternoon because I happen to like her, and not because she bought every stitch on my back," she said in a terrible anger.

"Okay, okay. Calm down," I heard him say but as the violence disturbed me I put down the extension.

"What a turd," she said when she came back into the

kitchen. "He never stops trying to mix me up in his business," she had just sat down when the telephone went again.

"That's him again. He's either thought of a new scold or else he feels that he's gone too far and wants to recover ground. It's not so easy for him as it was, since you—meaning another man—have come on the scene," she rose and took the receiver off the hook and left it off. She then made a light lunch and afterwards dressed very carefully, using silver jewellery and wearing a brown suede coat over her dress, and left to visit the hospital. I hung about the flat after she'd gone, putting the phone back on the hook, but she had not returned when I'd to leave for the five-thirty opening of the pub. It was one in the morning before I got home, if home it could be called. I noticed from the street that the lights in the flat were on, and when I opened the door she was sitting at the kitchen table.

"How was it? How is it that you're still up?"

"I saw Caroline in the hospital. She has cancer. Oh, there was no problem, she had the same marvellous manners, as if her only concern was to put me at ease, but she's dying. My father, typically, is trying to control her drinking. She had brandy while I was there, and she asked me not to tell my father. What a life it is. The old Portuguese servant Maria was there, we had coffee in a café afterwards, and she told me an extraordinary story. For months now Caroline hasn't been able to eat. My father would arrive at twelve, get Maria to make him a rare steak and salad, which he would eat in the kitchen, with a bottle of wine. Then at one he would dine with Caroline on the veranda and look at her with those moon-eyes and say, 'Sweetie I'm not able to eat anything either.' Afterwards Caroline would come into the kitchen and say to Maria, 'Isn't it terrible, Maria, poor Evatt isn't able to eat?' 'But how could he eat?' Maria would say to her. 'He's just had a rare steak and a bottle of wine,' but Caroline wouldn't hear, she'd go out murmuring, 'Poor Evatt.' By the way, you'll meet Maria, she's coming around. It's not easy for them, herself and the butler Mario, now that

Caroline's in the hospital. My father thinks they're idling and he's constantly trying to catch them out, finding all sorts of useless tasks for them. She says they'll soon have the silver worn with polishing.

"And then," she laid out banknotes on the table. "I met Pop at the hotel. He was all charm. I asked him for money."

"Why did you want to do that?" I asked her sharply but she only started to laugh.

"Part of the deal of getting me to Europe was that, late as it is, I would learn a trade, if interior decorating can be called a trade. So I'm going to work in the morning. For Pop. I said I thought it unfair to be using your money all the time. And right away he gave me this advance on earnings."

"I don't like it," I said. "We seem to be getting deeper and deeper in."

"He also warned me again that you must learn nothing about Caroline," she added. "It's partly vanity and partly a fear that you may be after loot, I guess, but tomorrow will be interesting."

"What I can't understand in the sense of loot is why he didn't marry Caroline, since you say he could have?"

"It's having your cake and eating it too. Caroline has the money but she is old. He thinks he's still a boy and wouldn't want to be so completely identified with an older woman," she yawned wearily as both of us realized how tired we were and had talked too long. "The only thing I have to add is that, much as I know about him, he really was great fun and spirit and charm at the hotel. The trouble with reflection is that it makes of everything—even life itself—a logical process."

"That may be just as well," I stroked her hair. "We'll go to bed."

The next night she was in bed but awake when I got back to the flat. "How did the first day working for your father go?" "It seems that I met you in the nick of time or I might soon be without a meal ticket," she said despairingly. "He's obviously sleeping with the secretary, and it's not a business, though of course they have clients and all that, it's just another extension of Pop's confusion: everything is run on a personal basis. What a fool I was to think I could learn any trade from him other than the oldest."

"Anyhow soon you'll be going to Dublin."

"It couldn't be soon enough. I'm sorry. I just feel lousy. You can't bathe in shit and come out smelling like a rose."

The servants began to visit the flat regularly, separately and together, the frail Mario who stammered, and the bawdy Maria, who even in an urban room looked rooted in some field. They came with gifts: chickens, rabbits, wines, fruit, and always stories, mostly of her father's doings. His present passion was for liver juice, and an enormous machine to extract it had come from Harrods. Old Maria laughed lustily, feet wide apart, as she told us.

"Why do they bring so many things?" I asked after Maria had left one evening.

"They hate the waste they see about them. Partly, too, it's an act of aggression against my father, since he treats them so abominably. They know Caroline is dying and instinctively they are already looking for new masters. We might even be the next government? We won't, but they don't know that."

"I seem to be always muttering it's a strange class of a life."

"Well, Buster, you better look sharp," she joked. "It's the only one you've got."

Often the father rang her but I was surprised very early one morning when she said, "It's Pop. It's you he wants to speak to."

"What does he want to speak to me for?"

"There is unfortunately only one way to find out," she said as she handed me the receiver with a mischievous smile somewhere between curiosity and amusement.

"You never seem to pick up the phone in that house," he opened aggressively.

"I don't like the telephone," I said and I could feel him give ground.

"Listen," he used my name in that familiar friendly

American way that I dislike, "I was wondering if just the two of us could get together soon. There are a few business matters I want to ask you about. Say, for dinner some evening soon?" he proposed, and I agreed to meet him the following evening at seven in the lobby of the hotel.

"Well, isn't that fascinating," she laughed outright at my dismay as I put down the phone. "Maybe he wants now to sell you the idea that the three of us should hit the sack together. Just one big h–a–p–p–y family. Or his little old self and you in a cosy twosome?"

"Oh for fuck's sake, lay off," I said and pulled her towards me.

I was early in the lobby and started to thumb through paperbacks on the stand while I waited. When he did come he approached the stand so stealthily that he took me by surprise. I guessed it was a practised ploy to win him the initial social advantage that had probably grown instinctive but it made me even more wary. He had a red twoseater outside the hotel that had been left running, and except for overweight and grey in his hair he looked much younger than his years at the wheel of the sports car. He had told me in the lobby he'd a table booked in the Chinese restaurant I'd eaten in on that first Saturday with my love, "It's very good though it's in the East End. Chinese diplomats go there," and since he didn't ask I didn't tell him I'd been there. He drove very fast through the city.

"Garlic Hythe, Bread Street, Leadenhall," he said as he drove, taking his eyes from the road to look full in my face as he spoke, "I love old streets. Think of the feet, the civilizations that walked those streets. They're not like new cities. They've been humanized." It made me smile because he sounded as if speaking out of one of his daughter's stories but I was wishing he'd watch the road instead of my face. Approaching Gardiner's Corner he farted. "That's an interesting smell," he looked me so full in the face that he had to swerve at the last moment out of the way of a truck.

"It's an East End smell," I said. "Probably from Tubby

Isaacs, jellied eels," I motioned towards Aldgate East Station where the eel barrow stood. I was determined not to allow an admission. I stared back at him in anger.

"Yes. It must be the jellied eels. It's a nasty smell," he rolled down the window and pretended to sniff the fumeladen air, my nervousness disappearing in anger as I watched him drive the dreary length of Commercial Road.

He had several small dishes in the restaurant and a large steamed fish for the main course. Once he snapped at the waiter over some dish but otherwise he concentrated on eating. There was no burden of conversation while he ate. I had no appetite and when he'd eaten the big fish he began to pick from my half-finished plates. I waited for him to ask me about Dublin or his business or to state in some way the reason for the dinner.

"A young man like you must know lots of girls in London?" I had heard and seen so much about him that nothing he said or did could surprise me now.

"I know one. Your daughter. That's enough." My one wish was to get quietly and quickly through the evening.

"There's this woman I'm crazy about," he continued. "She's in the design business. Her husband's a fool. He just takes care of the house. She had her second child last week. I'm so crazy about her that I could have speared her even when she was eight months gone. There's a bottle of champagne in the car. Why don't we go round to her with the bottle of champagne? I know she'd like you." He had put on spectacles to check the bill and pulled a wad of notes from his trouser pocket though it wasn't much more than half an hour since we first sat down. I thought of the many quiet hours she and I had spent over meals. "The fish was excellent," he said as he paid and added an extra coin to the tip.

"Well, what do you say?" he said on the street. "We'll take the bottle of champagne and go round. She lives in this nice house across the Heath in Hampstead."

"I won't this evening but thank you."

"Why not? The night's young yet."

"Maybe some other night but I said I'd go straight back to the Kensington place after dinner."

He glowered at me but got into the car. He was silent and drove very fast, yelling at other drivers. Coming close to Kensington he turned friendly again and when he saw the lights on in the flat he said, "Why don't we drop in on Isobel with the champagne?"

"But she's not expecting us."

"It's more fun that way."

"I wouldn't without warning. She may well be in bed already," though my tone was conciliatory it was firm.

"I don't understand you young people."

"You still have time to go round to see your friend."

"Maybe I have and maybe I haven't," he hissed and then, as I'd seen him do before, he turned all charm. He thanked me for a lovely evening and shook my hand, looking in my eyes as if I was the only friend he had in the world. I thanked him for the evening and waited until I saw the red car roar away before I opened the door.

"You're back very early?" she anxiously looked up from her reading.

"He ate very fast and I've just prevented him coming up to visit you with a bottle of champagne."

"Jesus. That's all I need after watching him horse and yell about the office all day. But how did you stop him? He's very hard to stop when he gets an idea like that into his head."

"I told him you might be in bed and that he couldn't come up and he saw I'd stick to that," and I began to describe to her the evening.

"The fart's typical," she said. "Often at Caroline's I saw him do it and get up and look around with a smile that said, 'I've done something naughty but wonderful.' And it's no surprise to me he didn't give any reason for the evening. Confusion is his natural element."

"I can't be rid of the whole mess quick enough," I felt soiled by the evening.

"It's selfish of me but I am glad you saw him at close

quarters. In that way I can be certain you know he's not just a fantasy of mine. He is almost unbelievable."

"After having dinner with him he's all too believable. Why don't we go for a walk? It's early yet."

Caroline died that night just after midnight. Maria rang up to tell us early in the morning. Maria and Mario had both been given notice already and the locks were changed on the Mayfair flat and valuable silver and tapestries removed. She had apparently died in the father's arms. He must have gone round to the hospital with the bottle of champagne after dropping me at the flat, I thought with malicious satisfaction, and it was the only way the death affected me.

Isobel didn't answer the phone when next it rang but went instead as usual to the office. As I was on all day at the bar I didn't see her until very late.

"That was some day," she was waiting up. "When I went into the office I discovered that everybody except the secretary and the old caretaker had already been fired."

"You'd think he'd wait till the woman was underground."

"Not him. Not when it comes to saving his own skin. You should see him. He's completely buoyed up. He's acting, he's busy, he's being decisive, he's bringing home the bacon for wife and kiddies. The servants were around," she indicated a pile of stuff in the corner of the room. Among it I noticed a few copper pots. "They were very depressed. They kept repeating the one word 'extraordinary' about my father's conduct. 'It's extraordinary Madam Isobel!'"

"Why did he change the locks and take out the valuables?" I asked as I idly bent to pick a tin from the pile of loot in the corner, it was a tin of pheasant soup in red wine.

"He'll try to hang on to everything, but he's pilfered so much over the years he can't be certain what action her heirs will take now that he can no longer count on her protection. And if he isn't able to hang on to the flat he still has the valuables. It's an extra line of defence."

"And have you been fired too?"

"No. I'm still useful. And there's another treat in store for you, my love. We've been summoned round to the matrimonial house for dinner the evening of the funeral."

"I don't believe it."

"You better believe it. It's another halfassed idea, a closing of the ranks, the united respectable happy family."

"If there is legal action won't you be one of the chief witnesses?" I asked quietly.

"Jesus. I never thought of that."

"We can't be too careful. I wish these servants hadn't brought us any of the loot."

We walked the same treelined avenue bringing irises to the dinner as on the first evening, crossed the squares of black and white marble, and descended to the great room opening on the garden. Both the father and stepmother met us at the foot of the stairs as before. They were both in a state of high elation.

"I was at this funeral today, in the country, at this great house. It was an old friend of the family. Someone who was very good to us," he drew me to the folding doors over whiskey, unable in his excitement to resist the desire to confide. "She was laid to rest in her rose garden, the servants carried the coffin. Wouldn't you think some of her family should carry her? Don't you agree that it was done in very bad taste? You would think a family like that should know better."

I thought: a sheet, a hole in the field, what did it matter; but I trotted out some cliché about how funeral customs varied. Still he kept harping on the servants bearing the coffin and wasn't satisfied until I agreed it was indeed probably in bad style. There were some unusually fine wines served with the meal of sole followed by roast duck, but fortunately his greed ensured that the meal wasn't prolonged and we took our leave as soon as it was possible.

"They think they're free now," she said to me quietly as we walked away. "She imagines she can enter now into the full respectability she has longed for. A tarnish has been removed. He is the boy playing hookey from the old parent. They imagine a new life is opening for them. But he had some nerve or panache or something or other to face the family in that rose garden."

"Would they not speak to him?"

"Are you kidding? They know the whole story."

"What now?"

"That's the real question," she replied even still more quietly.

There was not long to wait for the answer. A few nights later I came home at the usual hour from the bar to find her waiting up, "I thought you might be earlier," she reproached. "There was a big crowd in tonight. We just did the washing and had the usual nightcap and then I came." "I know. I was just hoping you'd come earlier." "What's up?" I asked.

"The euphoria's over. I had to meet Pop in the hotel. The suite of course is gone and the expense account. We had coffee in the lounge and he paid in cash, and he even made a call from one of the coin booths in the lobby. He's on an economy jag though he's taking his lawyer out to dinner tonight at the White Tower. He thinks he has everything covered legally but he's still scared that the heirs may sue. No, he was given nothing in the will—how could he be?—look at all she gave him or he took while she was alive? And I think that towards the end he wasn't finding it all that easy to get large sums from her. What he tried to tell me in the hotel today was that if there was a law case I'm involved in it as much as he is. 'Who paid for the analysis? Who paid for the clothes on your back? Who do you think bought you the flat?'—and there was a terrible row. I lost my temper. I told him you knew everything. And that you also said that, if anything, I had been exploited. He flew into a rage. 'I knew he was just a troublemaker from the first day. Maybe he's clever but he's just a cheap opportunist. When he discovers you have no money you'll find how long he'll hang around. *Then* who will back you up?'"

"You can be certain I'll be around for a very long time and you certainly won't ever need dear Pops to back you up again." I was too angry to say more.

His attack came at once. It took the form of a registered

letter, addressed to me, with a demand for a very large sum of money for the furnishing and redecoration of the flat. The demand was signed by him, with his name as well as the name of the late Caroline on the masthead. Also enclosed on separate paper was an itemized account of the sum demanded.

"What a bastard. I knew he'd make a dirty move, but not this. He's supposed to be setting me up, acting the good father . . . Now he just wants to get you out of the way."

"That won't happen and there's no use getting worked up."

"But we can't pay that sum. We haven't the cash."

"Maybe we have, maybe we haven't to pay the demand, but the first question is do you own the flat?"

"Of course I do. The flat was bought for me. It and the chance to learn a trade was why I moved here."

"But were you given deeds or anything? Just assurances won't cut much ice with a lawyer or bank manager."

"My father must have those," she was calmer.

"We certainly can't ask him for them."

"What can we do?"

"We'll have to get a lawyer."

Mr. Plowman gave me the name of a lawyer. He told me the lawyer was young and building up a practice and wasn't expensive. I used Plowman's name when I rang for an appointment. We found him at the hour of the appointment after walking several basement corridors in a large grey building in one of the narrow streets away from the law courts and towards the river. He wrote down all the facts and warned us to pay nothing till he had looked up the deeds of the flat.

The very next morning when the phone rang she put a hand over the receiver and said, "It's Pop. He wants you. Do you want to speak to him or not?" I nodded that I did.

"Well, you got my demand?"

"I did."

"Well what are you going to do? You haven't made any offer to settle it and you're still sitting in that apartment?"

"I can't pay a sum like that on demand. I'm trying to raise the money."

"You better make it snappy. Cash is pretty scarce on the ground just now. You may be interested to know that I've had to put all my Dublin interests on the market ..."

"I'll tell you within a week," I cut him short.

"Within a week," he tried to inject the words with venom. "Is Isobel still there?"

I motioned that he wanted to speak to her but she shook her head, "She says she doesn't want to speak to you," I said and put the phone down.

"Surely, you don't intend to pay him after what the lawyer said?" she asked incredulously.

"Are you joking? It's only to keep him off until the lawyer finds out one way or the other. We'll not know what we're doing till then;" and that word came within the week from the lawyer. She did not own the flat. It was in the name of a company called Icarus which was registered in her stepmother's name.

"I should have known," she said. "I feel I've been made a fool of so many times just because, stupidly, I wanted to trust him. And because I was always so grateful to see him pleasant and nice I'd give him the benefit of the doubt again, when I should have known that he could give nothing without being able to control it, without being able to take it away again. ..."

I saw she was upset and said, "Soon you'll be in Dublin and free of all this. It would have been nice to own this piece of property, it would have given us that much more freedom, but we have our lives, and that's more important. Look. There's some law that you have to be able to prove you've been resident for a certain number of days before you can get married in this country. Why don't we look into that today and get married before we leave for Dublin?"

We left the phone off the hook after that and about a week passed before her father played his last trick. He came round when I was at the bar. She described it to me when I got back.

"I was just sitting here, playing the radio, when the bell went. I expected no one at that time. I looked through the judas hole and sure enough there he was. For a second I wasn't going to open but then I thought he'll hear the radio anyhow and I might as well face it. He was all muffled up in cashmere scarf and camelhair coat, his best invalid act, worried and concerned, 'I've come to talk to you.' I just stood there and looked at him when he came in. 'Will you please turn off that thing, sweetie?' He was sweating. 'You're a woman of a certain age now and it's time you began to act reasonably. You must know by now that the affair with that Irish boy has gone on long enough. He may be very charming but he'll never be able to support you. Did you know that he works in a bar?'"

"How do you think he found that out?" I asked.

"He probably had you followed. But if I asked him how he found out it would have given him the advantage."

"What did you answer?"

"'I know he's working in a bar,' I said. 'He's working there for the year he took off from studying and teaching.' 'That may or may not be,' he hinted—the classical Pop one-two; if you can't get in the door try the window—you were no longer just after my nonexistent money. You were charming and irresponsible. Listen: 'Even if that's true, taking a year off studying and going to work in a bar shows a definite immaturity and lack of responsibility. You're grown up now and averagely intelligent'—thanks a lot, Pop, I felt like saying—'and it's time you began to act sensibly.

"'You know that money doesn't grow on trees. We all have to pull in our horns now and contribute. I'm selling out in Dublin and that small piece of property in Cheltenham. With that capital I'm going to set myself up in design. You have to keep too much staff in decorating. You could join in with me. That way you would acquire a real profession, a serious *métier*. What do you say, sweetie-darling?'

"'I'm listening.'

"'In the meantime, in order to have a secure income, the

plan is to rent the Mayfair place and this place,' he paused to wait for the effect.

"'I'm still listening', I forced him to continue and he was rattled."

"'You know how much room there is in the house in Holland Park. It's yours as well as mine. There's a whole separate apartment for you upstairs. You'll be completely independent. You can go and come as you please. As well, you'll have the backing of a family. It's time, you know sweetie, you started to think of settling down and having a family of your own. Most women of your age already have growing children.'

"'If this flat was bought for me why wasn't it put in my name?' It was my turn to attack.

"' Of course it's yours, sweetie,' he started to bluff. 'It's part of your inheritance.'

"'Why isn't it in my name then?'

"'It is in your name, sweetie. I don't know why you're being so difficult.'

"'It is *not* in my name.'

"'Oh yes. Well, that's because there turned out to be complex legal difficulties over foreigners owning property here. Putting it in the name of a company was a way around this,' I could see he was lying through his teeth.

"'I have to get ready to go shopping soon,' I warned him.

"'I'll send the van around tomorrow, sweetie,' he pushed, he looked quite crazy at that moment.

"'Don't bother. We're getting married next week and then we're moving to Ireland.'

"He went pale at first and then he began, 'You're out of your mind. You're crazy. You're just doing this because you hate me.'

"'I have to go shopping in a minute.'

"'You're doing this because you hate me,' he said, himself rigid with hatred. When he saw that nothing would have any effect he turned and padded down the stairs, slamming the outside door."

"I hope it was the last slam we'll hear. That it's really over this time."

"It is, love. There's nothing in it for him. He's played his last hand. He'll try to convince himself we never existed now."

I told them at the bar that I was going back to Ireland and at the same time asked Jimmy and Mr. Plowman if they'd witness the marriage. She had thought first of having Mario and Maria as witnesses but when last she saw them they were full of their new masters, as domestic animals secure in their new houses forget the old.

Much of the past came to disturb me as I prepared to go to the registry office and I was nervous. Phrases came, *Man born of woman shall endure for a time of trial here on earth in the hope of his eternal salvation,* and if I had not broken my link and was prepared to extend the blind chain there would have been music and a priest and altar and afterwards the images of aggression, shower of confetti and the battered kettle hurled after the bridal car; but she too had one day walked down the aisle looking the picture of death. Belief was as blind, I thought, as grief, one worn away by habit, the other becoming a habit. If I believed anything, and it was without conviction, it was that once upon a time we had crawled out of the sea and were making a circular journey back towards the original darkness.

"I felt matter of fact about the business until I heard him read out our parents' names, Pop's name and my mother's name, and your parents' names, your mother's profession as 'deceased'; then I got a bit of a start," she said as we left the building after the bare civil ceremony.

"It's like drowning," Jimmy said in his wry way. "You see your whole life in a flash."

"The one thing I got from the whole business is that it is all about property, which is amazing since we have so little of it," I had completely lost my early nervousness now.

"I must say, Patrick," Mr. Plowman said, "for the young lady's sake you might have risked a more colourful splash. It's the most sombre and functional ceremony it has ever been my privilege to attend."

"It's exactly what I wanted," she assured him.

"Well, what the ladies demand the ladies must get," he announced as he hailed a taxi to take us to the Boot and Flogger. We sat at a circular table at the back, its claws solidly gripping the floor, under the mirror sign of *The Vermin Remover to His Majesty*. As I had made it clear I was paying for the lunch, Plowman insisted on buying a bottle of champagne to begin with. We were toasted in Edwardian fashion, "To your health and prosperity and happiness! Will you take a glass with me?" Avocado and shrimp and a great bowl of salad, plates of cold beef and tongue, Stilton and Cheddar followed, and several bottles of the house claret and burgundy. Jimmy insisted on buying a bottle of 1894 port to end the meal. By this time he and I were making impractical and complicated arrangements, which in some way involved Liverpool, to meet after I had moved to Ireland, and I heard Plowman expounding the idea of a bar as a university to Isobel. If we ever got tired of Ireland, I heard him say, we must both come and work for him at the bar. We tried to read a letter in the window when we got outside, and at the line, *as my brother, Philip, in Acton, has a great want of wine,* Jimmy guffawed, and we all began to suspect that the best we could manage was to hail a taxi and get to our respective residences as quietly as possible.

We decided that I should go on first to Dublin, where I could look round for some temporary place for us to stay and make arrangements for resuming at the school. She would follow within a few days. The next week we went in to say goodbye to Mr. Plowman, and Jimmy came with us to Euston. We had a farewell drink in the station bar.

"I think the betting is heavily on the side of us being back in London before too long." I answered when he said how sorry he was to see us go.

"Why?"

I explained how there were two salary scales for teachers in Ireland: one for women and single men, and a higher for married men. If I applied to go on the higher scale they'd discover I wasn't properly married. If I remained on the single, which I'd have to do, they'd find out sooner or later in such a small city that I was living as a married man but not married. Either way I was certain to be fired.

"But you are married," he protested.

"Not in their eyes. Only marriage in their church counts for them."

"Why then didn't you get married in a church?"

"We couldn't. She was married before in a religious ceremony. They don't allow it a second time unless you can swing it with money—a lot of money. Anyhow I'm not sure we'd even want to if we could."

"It doesn't seem right to me that they can take a man's living away from him if he does his work properly just because he wasn't married in some bleeding church," he was the indignant, reasonable, gentle Englishman.

"The church controls the whole set-up there. Either you toe their line or you get out. I suppose it's the same in Spain."

"It beats me why you want to go back when you're practically certain you'll be fired within a few months."

I was going to say that as well as timidity there was some violence in my nature that demanded to see events through to their end, to be able to say it had to happen this way and no other, but I said, "I'd like Isobel to live in Ireland for a while and it's a way to do it," which was true as well.

"I suppose deep down everybody loves his own country no matter how bleeding awful it is," he reflected sentimentally, and we finished our drinks. The train was leaving in ten minutes.

"Well, it's nice to think you'll be back so soon even if it beats me why you're going," he smiled as we shook hands.

I walked through the narrow corridors, past rows of three-face-three compartments with the racks and scenic photos overhead, looking for an open carriage. The first I came to was the restaurant car. Through the glass I saw one passenger already eating at a window seat and a whitecoated waiter polishing something at the farther end. I was surprised to see them serving before the train began to move but thought it might be some official and I was even more surprised to find the door unlocked. When I had slid it half-open I saw with a shock of horror that the man eating by the window was no other than my father-in-law. As fast as I was able I got back into the corridor. My first thought was the shame of it; had he seen me run? Then I thought it couldn't be he at all; if it was in a lottery the chance of our meeting on this train must run to several millions, so it was most probably someone with a close physical resemblance. And after all I had more drinks than I was used to that day. I was so agitated that I went and sat in an empty compartment. If I do not face into the car, I started to think, I will spend a miserable night turning it over and over in my mind, dreading a chance meeting if I stirred on this train or the boat. All things in actual life, no matter how dreaded, are paltry compared with what the imagination can make of them and my imagination had been so obsessed with him and his moves over the last few months that probably for a while I'd be seeing him everywhere. Paralysed between my will to see and a natural flinching from unpleasantness I began to walk towards the car. I was no longer about to face her father or someone I mistook for him dining there but an embodiment in my mind of the violence and anxiety of the months that were over. I slid open the door and drew it shut again and walked slowly up between the tables. I still wasn't sure until he looked up from his plate. He uttered my name and with his hand invited me to sit opposite him, fixing me all the time with those great eyes: it was impossible to tell whether or not he was startled to see me.

"You should have the mixed grill. It's very good and simple. It's the only thing you can risk on these trains."

"How did you manage to get served before the train moved?" I found myself trembling as I asked but he relaxed at once, very pleased at the question.

"They say that money can't get you everything in this world but in my experience it can get you damned near everything. They know me on this train. I tip them well."

With a sudden jolt the train moved and rolled out of the station, gathering speed. "I recommend the mixed grill," he said, fixing me with his eyes, and I ordered the mixed grill and two beers.

"You can't order two beers," he said while the waiter stood at the table.

"Why not?"

"It's not done. It's impolite."

"I can order six beers if I want," my timidity fled. "Bring me three beers instead. It'll save your feet," I said to the waiter who was amused by the exchange and just nodded. Evatt glowered at the three beers when they came and his eyes rested longingly on the mixed grill but this time he didn't dare pick from the plate. Instead he called the waiter and ordered a second mixed grill.

"It's hardly very good form to order a second main course," I said between aggression and irony when the plate arrived but he only stared at me from under his eyebrows and fell to wolfing. There was no conversation while he ate. He had cleaned his second plate well before I finished.

"We got married last week. She's following me to Ireland in a few days," I said aggressively as he finished. It struck like a blow. The rushing air of the night filled the long silence. "Listen," he said. "I'd have sat here all the way to Liverpool and made polite conversation and never brought that subject up."

"Why should I make polite conversation when I know that subject's the first thing on your mind and mine?"

"She's crazy," he burst out. "She just did it because she hates me."

"She doesn't hate you. If anything she loved you too much. What's extraordinary is that it took so long for you to wear out that love."

He listened and was quiet for a moment. "She just means trouble. She's the one person that can hurt me. And I've got tired of getting kicked in the teeth all the time. I've cut her out of my will. She'll not get a cent. There's a limit to the number of kicks in the teeth a person can take," he seemed to grow larger across the table as if he was inflating himself with his own rhetoric.

"It's just as well for her she's cut out. There's something squalid about hanging round waiting to fill dead shoes. She's better attending to her own life."

He slumped into a smaller shape again, scared by the coldness.

"She's crazy, even keeps saying she had nothing to do with Caroline when she was in it just as deep as I was. She forgets where every stitch of clothes on her back comes from . . ."

"She was offered things and she accepted them and she never sought to take advantage of your rich woman. In fact she was fond of her and sometimes upset by your treatment of her. She's as deep as I am in it and you know how deep that is."

He was furious. Again the ball of his ego puffed itself out like angry fur. "You're just a liar and a troublemaker. I knew you were at the root of all the trouble."

"We can very easily discover whether I'm a liar or not. We can go and ask her."

"I repeat: you're a liar and troublemaker and why don't you get out."

"You forget we're married."

"She can get a divorce. I'll pay for it," he was blind.

"That's her business and mine, not yours. And I said it can be easily proved whether I was lying or not. We can go to her."

"I won't go to her. Why should I go to her? I'm a big man. I'm not a small man."

"And I suppose the way you married her off the first time without giving her any choice is a lie too?" And the puffed ball went down again. It struck, as the first blow of our marriage.

"I was acting for what I thought was the best."

I saw clearly for the first time how there was no centre to

his mind if mind it could be called. It was all blind instinct. He lived off others, what reactions he caused, what advantages he could force. I saw clearly too how he could only work in confusion. If he was cornered in one place he'd just abjectly back down and start a hare up somewhere else.

"And then the abortion you arranged in Switzerland. Is that a lie too?"

"I just did what I thought was best."

"Did it ever dawn on you that she should have had some say in the matter? You might decide it was best for someone to be dead and where would that lead?"

"She hates me but I was acting for the best."

"She doesn't hate you. She thinks that both businesses were in the long run lucky for her."

"I was acting for the best," he repeated and I saw he was close to breaking. I had no feeling whatever for him now but I saw that if he had to take any more punishment he would break. I switched the conversation to his reason for going to Dublin. At once it was as if all that had gone before had never been spoken. He was going to sell off his Dublin property. He was staying at the Russell. Why didn't I drop by for a drink?

"I'm going to concentrate on London. I'm shaking the dust of Dublin and Cheltenham off my feet," he said aggressively.

Chains of light ran by the windows. Often a lake of light would glow in the sky. All of England will be one big city soon, I thought.

"I think I'd like a beer," he said and looked round for the waiter. The car was now full. He couldn't catch the waiter's eyes.

"I see what you mean about those beers," he snarled.

"Have this can?" I said. "You can drink from the can till we get the waiter," and I pulled the metal seal loose by its ring. We had two more beers later and we paid separately for what we'd had as the train wound into Liverpool. He tipped heavily, but it was somehow wrong, a confusion or ambiguity about whether he was serving the waiter or the waiter serving him, and the waiter just pocketed the money, and as he said the formal "Thank you," showed neither pleasure nor displeasure. Normally I would have taken the station bus to the boat but he insisted I ride with him in a taxi. As he was going first class we separated at the entrances but arranged to meet afterwards on deck. We watched the ship move slowly out through the locks.

"Don't you love ships and these old locks?" he said predictably. "In an aeroplane you're just flushed from one hole to another. This way you feel the slow beauty of time."

I agreed, turning away so that he couldn't read my face. *O Lord in Thine house are many mansions,* I thought and remembered his daughter saying he couldn't purchase a spool of thread without embroiling himself with the seller.

"She doesn't hate me," he suddenly said, fixing me with those big eyes.

"No. She doesn't hate you," I answered and before it could go further I said I was tired and was going below to sleep.

When I got to the cabin I undressed and climbed up the wooden ladder. I tried to read but wasn't able. My mind enfevered still with the violence of the incongruous evening, often leaping back from its broken pieces to the words of my love. Only towards morning did I sleep and I hadn't decided whether to leave the ship as soon as it docked or wait till everybody had gone ashore to avoid the embarrassment of another meeting.

I rang Lightfoot from the large basement restaurant in Cathedral Street where I had breakfast. He was surprised till I explained that I'd come over on the nightboat, that my leave from the school was up the following week. He asked me if I'd a place to stay for the night and told me I could stay at their house until I found a place. We arranged to meet at the Stag's Head after he'd finished work. He'd take the car so that there'd be no trouble in getting my bags to the house.

I went that same morning to the school. The headmaster was delighted to see me. The old man who'd filled in for me for the year had been much absent because of illness and the class had fallen behind.

"You have your work cut out for you, *a mhaistir*. They're in need of a firm hand. Their noses will have to be kept hard down to it for the whole year for them to catch up," and he'd have had me begin there and then except I pleaded the excuse that I'd arranged to visit relatives in the country. Finally it was agreed I'd resume on the actual day I was due back. "It's great to see you back in the breach, *a mhaistir*," he beamed as we shook hands.

"That's a surprise," Lightfoot said when I told him I was married. The eyes held that same glow of passionate amazement with which he looked at everything but they had long ceased to be surprised by anything that came into their view. When we had taken the bags back to the house and we had eaten, the mother suggested that Isobel should stay in the house when she came until we found rooms.

I was as happy as a broken limb miraculously made whole again as I saw her step on the gangplank of the boat in three days. She was incredulous at first when I told her of the chance meeting on the train.

"It must have been a nightmare for him. Nobody ever spoke to him like that before, and I'm so glad you said I loved him, because it was true."

"He's probably got the whole meeting well shut out or rationalized by now," I said.

"Of course. But I wonder if conscience can be shut out that effectively all the time?"

The next morning, Sunday, we walked in the path of the dead across the hill of Howth, and if the only true festivals are festivals of the spirit it was the end of the honeymoon of our love before our life in Ireland began.

We had a plate of shelled prawns and brown bread with our second glass of stout in the Tavern and then we found ads for rooms in a glass case outside a newsagents. We wrote down the addresses and went round knocking on the doors but all the rooms we saw were either too expensive or too awful or we didn't like the owners or they didn't like the prospect of us.

"It seems a lost cause to me," I said, depressed by the tramping and so many faces and so many rooms we'd never live in, "Why don't we just go and sit by the front?"

"Why don't we have one last try. I'd love to live out here," she looked at the list, a line through all the addresses except two or three low down.

We turned away from the front to a street of fishermen's cottages, their roofs and chimneys as steps of an irregular stairs climbing uphill. A little woman in black opened the door. The room she showed us was cheap and very small, a tap dripping into a small cracked sink, a gas fire under the mantel, a bed in the corner, a gas stove on tottery legs inside the door, a table covered with lino that had red and white squares, three chairs crowding the rest of the room.

"Can we think about it?" I asked.

"There are others coming to look at it later this evening," she pressed.

"I'll let you know in a few hours . . ."

"Of course you know I can't hold it."

"I know that."

"Well?" I asked as we walked downhill, away from the closed door.

"Is there need to ask?" she said sharply, exasperated too by the hopeless trudge from door to door. "It's a slum room."

"There are people who have to live in such rooms," I answered her sharpness with a borrowed aggression.

"Let's not quarrel. Let's go to the front," she said quickly.

"Let's go to the front then."

We walked far out on the pier wall and sat on rocks close to the harbour light. We watched the waves break against the rocks and two boys row clumsily in the choppy tides between us and Ireland's Eye. Their oars often missed their stroke so that the blades constantly skimmed up splashes of spray.

"Do you feel you took on too much taking me back to Ireland with you?" the words fell so quietly as she stared out at the sea.

"What do you mean?" I asked in sudden agitation.

"What I said. I want you to feel free. It may be all too difficult and if it is you mustn't feel any responsibility to me."

"But I love you," I said out of the shadow of losing her.

"Yes, but I don't want to force anything. With that love I want fairness between us. An equal relationship."

"Is it that the life and rooms here like the last slum room may be too poor for you?" I said bitterly and with some anger.

"No, no, love. It's not the rooms. I was afraid you might feel you had to go through with what will be difficult out of a sense of duty or responsibility to me now that I've come here and I don't want you to feel that. I'd prefer to lose you before that. That's all I wanted to say. My interest in our marriage is as selfish as yours."

For a moment we were as separate from one another as we were from the sea chopping against the blocks of granite below us, as separate from one another as we would be in our future deaths. Out of the pain of that knowledge a fierce yearning for her came that was almost grief.

"Why don't we get a bus into town and eat and have a drink or go to the picture? After all the tramping we need some excuse or other to celebrate at last."

"That's a good idea," she laughed as she got up from the rock smoothing back her hair, but as we went back down the long pier to the bus stop on the front she said, "Soon, soon, though, we'll have to try to find some place of our own, any place. In the States they say house guests and fish stink after two days."

Searching round Howth on my own for rooms the next day I saw Mr. Cotter, the vegetable man. He was counting change from a leather bag that hung from his neck into a woman's hand in a doorway, the pony patiently flicking at flies by the railing gate. We'd used the same local before I went away. Each night he stabled his pony in the pub yard. He rented the stable for some small sum from the people who owned the pub. After he'd stabled and foddered the pony he'd climb the stairs to the lounge, touch his hat at the door in an old courtesy to the barman and drinkers; the barman would lay his large brandy on the counter, which he'd swallow quickly as if for warmth, and spent the next hour over two slow bottles of stout. As soon as the towels were draped on the pump handles he'd leave, touching his hat on the way. He had to be up for the market at six. The old brown pony, I remembered, wore a rug in winter.

I waited by the pony at the gate watching him count out the last of the change, touch his hat to the woman, and as he turned the pony started to move to the next gate, where it waited for him to follow, the old wooden scales hanging from the back of the cart. We shook hands and passed sufficient polite remarks for me to ask him if he knew if any of his customers had rooms to rent. He replied at once that he did: a Mrs. Logan, the last of her daughters had been married in June, there was only herself in the house with her husband now. I wrote down the address and as we parted he touched his hat and told me to say that he had sent me. He started to weigh turnips on the scales as soon as he had joined his cart.

There was a long lawn inside the iron railing on the seafront, a gravel path round a single laurel bush to the granite steps up to the door. A short stocky man in a blue business suit and open-necked white shirt answered my knock. He waited aggressively with one hand on the halfopen door for me to state my case as if he thought I was a door-to-door salesman.

"Mr. Cotter the vegetable man sent me. He said you might be willing to rent me rooms."

"Come in," he said abruptly. "You'll have to see the missus about that. She looks after that. She's shopping but she's due back any minute."

He showed me into a room to the left of the hall, it was a front room, covered sofas and armchairs and a carpet that was faded but little worn, wedding and baptismal photos on the walls with Jesus and the Virgin. A stuffed parrot stood under glass on the marble of the mantel and by its side a tall grandfather clock that no longer ran and had once told the phases of the moon and tides. From the comic moonface under the hands in the first quarter it must have stopped when the moon was full at the low spring tides, one of the clear nights they hunt along the sands at the turn of the low tide for bubbles of the razor fish with buckets and with knives.

"She'll be back any minute. She has to be back for me to go to Hughes for the evening paper," he said and left for the opposite room across the hall. Through the angle of the halfopen door I saw him sit at a small table on which a book was open. He sat very rigid, with one hand resting on his forehead, and he seemed to leaf through the pages very quickly. I next heard him light a cigarette and I could smell the tobacco from where I sat. To pass the time I had started to examine the moon and tides on the clock when she came through the halldoor with a shopping bag in a flutter of little cries. She was small too but perfect-featured in a frame of white hair. I shook her hand and since the husband made no move from the table answered her smile of enquiry with, "Mr. Cotter sent me. He said you might be willing to rent me rooms." Her smile was full of kindness but without watchfulness or intelligence.

"Mr. Cotter is nice. He's been coming to me over twenty years. A real old gentleman. He charges a bit higher than the shops but he brings it to the door and you can be sure what you're getting is fresh."

"He said you might have rooms?" I interrupted.

"I told Mr. Cotter about the rooms. And he said if he heard of someone quiet looking for rooms he'd send them to me. People said put an ad in the paper but you don't know what you're getting from an ad," and she started to tell me about the weddings of her daughters that had left her with the vacant rooms. I told her I was a schoolteacher as we eventually climbed the stairs to the rooms.

She at once rattled off the names of four teachers who lived on the road. She had gone out with a schoolteacher before she had the misfortune to run into old Johnny jumpup humped over the book downstairs. There was another teacher, but I found I didn't have to listen, and that she didn't even look for the barest of responses. The two rooms had good simple furniture and were clean. There was a full view of the harbour from the front room and at night, she said, you could hear the sea. I asked her the rent. The sum she named was very small. I told her I'd take the rooms if she'd have me and asked if she'd like to meet my wife before deciding, "She didn't feel well and didn't come with me today."

"If Mr. Cotter sent you I'm sure you'll be all right," she was anxious to be rid of the decision. "Sure, you can take the girl out so she can see for herself anyhow."

"We'll come about the same time tomorrow then."

"Is she a Dublin girl or from down the country?" she asked on the stairs.

"She's American," I answered uneasily.

"O you blackguard, I suppose one of our Irish girls wasn't good enough for you," she gave me a playful push.

"It wasn't that."

"I suppose it was love then," she laughed at the door. "'Ah love,' my mother used say. 'Love, is it, daughter? Sure love flies out the window.'"

I thanked her and said goodbye.

"Old Johnnyjumpup has gone for the paper," she said as I went down the granite steps. "He lives for that bloody old paper."

She waved to me as I closed the gate and since I liked her I felt uneasy and guilty about my feeling that she was another stupid sister of mine in Christ or whatever shadow or constant we find, as the door finally closed.

"Do you think it will be long before they find out at the school we're not married in the church?" she asked a little anxiously on the bus on our way to look at the rooms in Howth the next day.

"It's a chance but sooner or later they will."

"Then we'll have to leave?"

"That's right."

"How do you think they will find out?"

"The old letter of freedom, and the single scale you heard me tell Jimmy about at Euston. They'll check once they find out we're living together."

"They'll fire you then?" She seemed to be repeating the worst in order to find confidence.

"That's right."

"Why did you come back then?" her nervousness was gone and she was asking in the calm that is reflection.

"Out of obstinacy," I began but when I saw her seriousness said, "You remember when we talked of suicide and you told me that when you were going through that horrible time with your father if it continued for two more years you would end it."

She nodded, "It would have been a pity because I always felt that with any luck I could live a reasonably decent life, but it's true I had more or less set a limit."

"I'd never do it for this one reason. I have no idea where my life comes from or where it will go—probably back into nothing—but to take it would seem to me to make some judgement on it. I don't know enough to judge. I know nothing, and so I'll see it through like any natural imbecile. The same with the school. Let *them* sack me. I didn't make the rules. It's almost certainly no more on my part than stupid male aggression, but that's what I feel."

"It doesn't seem imbecilic to me, it's a way, but it wouldn't be my way," I felt my aggression even harsher in the face of her gentleness.

"Probably the meaning of all that guff is that I want just to live with you in Ireland for a time," I grew ashamed and embarrassed of my big words. "Look—the harbour."

The bus had turned the corner into Howth. "It's the next stop," I said and we scrambled downstairs.

Mrs. Logan showed both of us the rooms as uninhibitedly as she'd showed them to me the day before and we arranged to move in the next day. We had almost a week of quiet mornings and meals and walks, and drink and talk in the evenings, before I'd to return to the school the next Monday.

The bell echoes down the corridors as it passes from door to door and the children smile at me as they put away books and comics. It is the last time I'll hear that bell.

"If every day was as easy as today it'd be nice coming to school," an outgoing child tells me, and it crosses my mind to tell him that it is my last day, but I do not.

"*Seasaigi. In Ainmanathair,*" I begin to bless myself and we chant our gratitude for the day, the last day, "*Cle, deas, cle,*" down the clanging corridor to the back entrance. I see the bus edging its way through the hordes of children let loose and I jump on and climb to the top deck. That way I have avoided all meetings.

Pushing for the same bus a Friday evening years before comes for no reason to my mind and meeting the inspector at the gate. "It must be great to have the weekend in front of you, *a mhaistir,*" he stopped me. "Yes but I look forward to coming back to the work on Monday," I blush still as I hear the slavish caution of my whole forever overmastered race in my voice. "When I was a young teacher I could hardly wait for the weekends," he gave me in his paternal voice right to the enjoyment of the weekend: and on the bus I think what flotsam the mind stores and this day at least I have some pleasure in shaking off some of that slavishness from my feet.

Several times on the bus that morning returning to the school I felt like getting off and taking the next bus back to Howth and packing for the nightboat to London. I'm glad this day in the classroom I stayed and saw it through. I'll never have to imagine what it might have been if I hadn't seen it through. It happened this way and no other way.

The concrete on the low roof and the nineteenth-century mansion beyond and the milling bodies on the concrete were, with a shock, the same as I remembered them that first day back. I heard my name called by children as I pushed my way through and if they were close I put out a blind hand of recognition on some head of hair.

"The stranger is back. Welcome back the stranger," the jocular cry went up as I entered the staffroom. In a halftrue, halfsimulated confusion of emotion I shook hands, and as I bent to sign the book the bell rang out on the concrete. In the silence the noise of a stubbing of a cigarette on the ashtray and Tonroy's frail laugh, "Well lads, I suppose it can't be helped." The bell rang again in the silence and was followed by a rush of feet. The lines were forming.

"Well, the holidays are over. Good times are bad times. You should never have come back," Boland gave me a playful push as we straggled out on the concrete. "I bet you it was pretty hot over there."

"Well, hotter than this morning anyhow," I answered.

"See you later," he sported a roguish smile and a generous wave of the hand.

"*Cle, deas, cle, deas, cle,*" I heard the boots march in time. "*Rang a tri, rang a se, rang a ceathar. Gluasaigi. Cle, deas, cle,*" the boots and voices beat into one another as the headmaster, his hand on the tongue of the bell, hurried the classes to their rooms. It was as if I'd never been away.

"*Failte romhat arais, a mhaistir,*" he smiled and touched me on the shoulder as I paused. "See you later, *a mhaistir,*" he added but he didn't let up a moment in the drilling of the classes towards the rooms and I had to hurry after mine. Down the corridor they went. "*Cle, deas, cle.* Stand for the prayers. Sit down. Open the roll book. Good children after the holidays. Call out the names."

"*Micheal O Briain,*" my Gaelic was awkward after a year's disuse.

"*Annseo.*"

"*Padraig o Loingsign.*"

"*Annseo.*"

"Who'll take this to the office?" I asked when I finished, a picture of any school morning, and the hands shot up, "Me, me, sir, me," a charming version of their later life. "First in, first sitting down, first with his desk open, first with his book out," the little Cockneys used to compete in the London school.

I hurriedly handed the book to a boy in the first seat and hurried him out before he had time to gloat. As soon as he returned I started to teach. In the first hours of teaching before it settles as a habit it is easy to see the classroom as a microcosm of everywhere: to those that have it shall be given; from those who have not it shall be taken away, as the clever hunt after knowledge and the faces of the dullards cloud. I had forgotten how long I'd been teaching when with a knock the headmaster was in the doorway. He was all smiling, rubbing the backs of his hands instead of stroking the bald head as he did when he was uneasy or tense.

"I see you're *go dion* at it already, *a mhaistir,*" he beamed approval.

"Might as well take the plunge at once," I relaxed in the room the cliché gives.

"Ah well, the first day is no more than the breaking of the ice."

I saw he wanted to talk with me and gave them reading so that they'd be still.

"Well, *a mhaistir*, we'll be expecting great things from this class after such a long holiday of fine weather," he said to the class, his arms folded.

"Certainly, *a mhaistir*," I echoed him as I went to join him at the window, the rust of autumn already on the three beech trees after the dry summer.

"Well, how did you find our colleagues across the water?"

I started to tell: the obsession with rules and regulations, the wormwood of class distinction and I grew ashamed of my own voice in its general clichés and thought of little Clapson who taught next door to me, tank mechanic in the Sahara, "We never were in much danger as we moved behind the lines. The worst was the sand and the stink of flesh in the burntout tanks. You could hear the flesh sizzle in the hot metal." His wife who typed at Yardleys; the cold ham and lettuce and the timber paling at the end of the garden. Small and grey and infinitely gentle with the children and lacking confidence in the work he did so well because he'd come to teaching through the backdoor of the army. It was an obscenity to place him in some generality. I waited in the hope of not having to continue but his face beamed eagerness.

"What about corporal punishment?" it was unthinkable to him that I would have done anything else other than teach while in London.

"It's more or less abolished."

"But what do you do with a right bad egg?"

"You can send him to the headmaster, who'll give him a little homily, and he'll come back grinning. If you send more than one a week the headmaster'll soon get fed up with you and you'll be accused of being inefficient. The theory is that all children are supposed to be basically good. Your job is to draw it out."

"You think that?" he asked, at once suspicious that I'd been indoctrinated with some fashionable heresy while away.

"No," I laughed.

"They're trying to bring in that idea too here. The poor teacher has to be cureall. They have their jails and bread and water but if the teacher has to punish *he's* to blame. Who's to blame for the criminal?"

"They say society," I was glad of the turn of the conversation away from the personal.

"But who's society?"

"Everybody and nobody," I laughed in the play.

"Precisely, *a mhaistir*," he argued heatedly. "They throw all the blame over on the poor teacher. He's guilty if he doesn't begin their utopia. And you'll get the one bad egg in the classroom just as well as in the outer world."

I loved his narrow passion, faithful to the person that he was; so alien to my uncertainty, but was glad when he looked at his watch.

"And now that you've gone like Caesar—*veni, vidi, vici*—where would you prefer to teach?" he changed to his affable self.

"In Ireland," he beamed in the sun of my choosing, he was Ireland.

"Ah, hills are green far off. Though when you put in for

that leave of absence I supported you."

"I was very grateful for that."

"Let him go, I said. He's young. It's natural to hanker when young. He'll see for himself and when he comes back he'll be settled. When he's married he'll not be able to go. And speaking about that, *a mhaistir*," he changed from the affable to the jocular, "Are you any nearer to giving us the big day?"

"No, *a mhaistir*," I hated my own unease, though the embarrassment was natural and he'd not notice.

"Sooner or later, *a mhaistir*, like everybody else you'll get your head in the noose."

I remembered a hot Saturday in summer a few years before I went away. I'd come in the evenings to help him prepare the ground for sport's day by scything the long grass and nettles on the edges and when the light had failed and we had put away the tools he'd said, "That was a great help, *a mhaistir*. You must come back to the house with me for a cup of tea." "It's late and I don't want to trouble Mrs. Maloney," I'd tried to escape but he was insistent. I walked with him down the treelined avenue to his house and close to the gate he paused, "I see the brother-in-law's car here. Now, *a mhaistir*, you're welcome to the tea but I won't drag you in if you don't want."

He explained awkwardly that he'd been at the school since early morning, had missed all his meals, living on milk and figrolls, and had brought me home as a buffer against his wife's possible anger over the spoiled meals. Now that his brother-in-law was there I was no longer needed.

"I'll leave it to another time then, *a mhaistir*," I was glad to be released.

"Women are fine but they don't understand some things. That's what you'll have to put up with when you're married too," he said as he wished me goodnight. It was three years ago, three years of a life gone.

"Ah well, I won't hold you up any longer but I wanted to tell you you're welcome back," he said in the same voice that first day I'd come back and smiling at the door he turned to the class, "I'm expecting great things from these lads this year, *a mhaistir*," and smiling still with a diffident little wave of the hand backed out the door.

I got through lunch more easily than I'd expected—the kettle boiling on the red ring, the big aluminium teapot with the black handle on the stand in the centre of the table, the paperbags or plastic boxes that held their sandwiches beside their cups and saucers. For a little time they questioned or teased me about London but soon they turned to the spent holiday and their own cares.

I had to smile as I watched the quiet James keep his head low over his sandwiches through all the questioning. In the green egotism of my first days in this staffroom I had tried to turn the conversation to ideas and poetry, away from the continual talk of salaries or what had happened that morning in the classroom or what had been on TV the night before.

"Why didn't you support me? You know better than that?" I accused him an evening I called at his house and we'd gone to the pub and talked.

"What?" his eyes opened wide with amazement behind the thick lenses. "I certainly don't want to have them on my back. I was going to tell you not to be trying to drag me into those arguments."

"Surely, they can talk about more than *Dangerman* or the status of teachers. They're supposed to have some education."

"Arrah, it's young you are. Up to their elbows they want to be in the big fat greasy pot of life. And anything that rocks that same greasy pot will soon get quick corrected."

I had argued with him then but now had come full circle to his view; and now would curse a newcomer for a fool if he disturbed the even flow of banality at the table with ideas or poetry.

"It can't be helped. It must be done," Boland got jocularly up halfway through the break to relieve Tonroy on the concrete who came in rubbing his hands, "Nothing like a good cup of tea after that mob," and soon a last bell was clamouring for us all on the concrete.

"Well, it's the last lap," I heard someone say as we straggled out to the lines, Maloney sending some of the lines marching ahead of us to the rooms the moment we appeared in the doorway.

"It wasn't as bad as I imagined," I told Isobel as soon as I got to the rented rooms that first day back at the school, "but it's a relief to get off the bus and see the boats and the sea and walk to these rooms."

As I leave the school a last time in the old 44A I know the world of the school will be soon as far away as that world of her father, becoming only presences in the mind, and even the mind itself will one day go. It is a kind of joy to face that and know it and let that go too. Overhanging branches hit against the top deck windows at the empty tennis courts beside the church in Seafield Road. In a few days we'll be in London. We'll build our changing lives together outside the father and the world I now leave. All things are relative except our death, and seen in its shadow even the dismissal of this day borrows some of the graveclothes of the absolute, and must wear them in that dignity they acquire from having undergone the ultimate indignity.

I get off the bus at a sandwich place on the front. I take the milk and sandwiches to the part of the counter along the window where I can stare out over the speeding cars to the reclaimed greensward and the sea wall and then the sea, the tall chimney of the gas works smoking the other side of the bay. My ordinary extraordinary day is almost ended. I have two hours to enjoy until I meet Lightfoot in the Stag's Head to say goodbye. I meet the priest at night. And afterwards I go home to my love in the room at Howth. The consciousness of doing even very small things for the last time brings to them its poignancy. The gulls' shadows will not float this evening on the concrete. The sky has filled. I can see it is already raining out on the bay.

Those first months in Mrs. Logan's rooms at Howth passed

in that quiet happiness that cannot be described. Each Friday when the bell rang at three was miracle hour. I'd have all that evening and all of Saturday and all of Sunday to be with her. We went for walks on the hill and along the sea, went to cinemas and pubs, talked or were rich in one another's silence, safe in the luxury that we could break that silence to eagerly seek one another again, free as well to return to silence when we tired of the inherent impossibility of finding much except the need again for silence in our seeking.

Out of loneliness and boredom Mrs. Logan came sometimes to the rooms.

"He's in love. He thinks he hasn't got you. Ah, but as my mother used say, 'Is it love you're talking about, daughter, love is it, sure love flies out the window,'" and she'd tell some long story of her childhood and what the fishmonger and Mrs. Byrne said to her that morning and what she said to them.

"Mrs. Byrne went with Maureen Connolly to Arnott's the week before the wedding. They'd finished when Mrs. Byrne said, 'What about a nightdress for the wedding night?' And didn't she turn round brazen as brass and say she didn't need any nightdress. She said that's old hat now. Apparently she intends to sleep with him in her birthday dress. Trothon, there's certain parts of me my old Johnny never laid eyes on to this day. If you let them know everything they just walk over you," but she didn't demand to be listened to. She'd stand and talk herself out and when she'd tire she'd leave with a touching laugh, "You've had your fill from this old one."

The husband's day revolved round the morning and evening papers and his library books. He never gleaned anything from these books, as far as I could observe, turning the pages as prayer wheels. Odd informations stuck. Somerset Maugham was his favourite author. They shared the same aversion: when he was walking out with his wife he always hated it when she'd take his arm and he had read in the Autobiography how Somerset Maugham hated anybody to take his arm too.

Lightfoot was the only other person we saw because of the

need to keep our marriage secret, and this lack of any social life became a growing constraint. There was the exasperation of having to cover up at the school with small lies; it didn't seem worth the indignity of lying, and sooner or later I knew they were certain to find out anyhow. So when the truth finally got out it came as a relief.

What a small country Ireland is, where everybody who is not related knows someone who knows someone else you share an enemy or friend with. A shopping Saturday Mrs. Logan ran into Jones's wife in Henry Street, Jones the immaculate little cock of the concrete schoolyard. They had coffee in Arnott's.

"By God you're a sly one. I ran into Mrs. Jones in Henry Street. I used to know her mother in the old days in the East Wall, and she tells me her husband teaches with you, and they didn't even know you were married. But God that's the slyest way to do it I have ever heard of. I wish I and my old Johnny had thought to get it over so nice and sly in our day," she rattled on, too stupid to even suspect anything wrong, and gave me a full description of Mrs. Jones's family in the old days on the East Wall.

"The game's up at last," I said to Isobel when I escaped to our rooms. I told her what I had just heard from Mrs. Logan in the hallway. "Jones never liked me. They'll have the dogs out at once."

"Will we leave at once then?"

"No. I'll see it through this time to the last amen," I smiled as I shook my head.

"But there's the indignity and it will be unpleasant," she hinted.

"It'll not be very pleasant for them either. And once I've seen it through I won't have to think about it anymore. It happened this way and no other. And I can wash my hands then."

A local priest came to the house the very next evening. He interviewed both Logans behind the closed door of the big rooms downstairs that held the stuffed parrot and the great clock that had once told the phases of the moon and the tides. He left without asking to see us. When we saw the Logans on our way out for a walk after the priest had gone they were plainly confused and embarrassed but they showed us no hostility.

"The local curate was sent round to check. Their style's to act by stealth. Even for them it's getting dangerous to display their power too obviously. Now that they've checked they'll move tomorrow in the school," I said as we began to walk towards the pier wall. I was grateful for the Logans' lack of any hostility but disliked seeing them so embarrassed. I decided to explain to her what was wrong when we got back. He was reading the same library books behind the open door of the front room and I could feel his intense listening to my steps as I came down the stairs. I turned up the hallway and knocked on the closed kitchen door. She was more tense and frightened than I was, which made first words difficult. I told her we were legally married but that in the eyes of the church it was not lawful. I'd be almost certainly fired from the school, we'd be leaving fairly shortly but if it was any real embarrassment for her to have us stay we'd leave at once.

"Sure, love, what'd I be doing putting you out? You never caused any trouble in this house. I don't see why people want to go causing trouble. At least you married and did the decent by the girl, didn't you?" and she went on. The husband had been following our every word from the front room and now joined us in the kitchen. He turned out to be rabidly anti-clerical, an opinion no doubt acquired from the breadth of his reading, which he liked to think of as somehow dangerous but most certainly he never expressed it near the presence of a priest. "A crowd of bowsies in black," was his phrase. I withdrew before the Logans began to dispute with one another over the church. I was very grateful to them and never felt as close to them as now when we were about to leave their rooms.

The harsh gull shriek mingled with the beat of small feet marching on the concrete, *Cle...deas...cle...cle,* that next day I felt a tug on my sleeve: it was Maloney, like a knob on a turbot the bump of the cane protruded beneath the padded shoulder of the suit, "*Go mba leathsceal, a mhaistir,* but could you drop into the office for a few minutes after school?" his voice trying to be casual was tense.

"It's no trouble, *a mhaistir,*" I nodded agreement.

"*Gura maith agat, a mhaistir,*" he stroked his shining head with his palm.

"*Gura maith agat, a mhaistir,*" I knew my days on the concrete were numbered.

After school I knocked on the door of the office. There was no answer. I saw Maloney come hurrying towards me down the corridor in a jangle of keys. He unlocked the door, "I won't be a minute, *a mhaistir.* Just make yourself comfortable." It was an old technique of his with angry parents. "They get frightened alone in the office. They come in like roaring lions but by the time they're ten minutes waiting for you they turn meek as mice. Putty." I did not sit in the big chair facing his across the littered table but went to the window; the beech tree, the nineteenth-century mansion, the daws on the roof, and the iron stairs of the fire escape, my love's dark head in that window once. I smiled ironically as I turned away. How many different forms had that love by now taken, by how many different names had I called to her, and yet I was calling still, the room in Howth now. . .I looked at my watch. He would keep me exactly ten minutes. One door of the cupboard was open, roll book, reports, tubes of gum, ink, erasers, exam papers, a splintered cane in the corner. Are there any beautiful rooms in Ireland? "Rooms need care and love as much as people to be beautiful," I had heard her say once. He came in exactly the ten minutes, rubbing his hands, smiling, "I'm sorry to keep you so long, *a mhaistir.*"

"It's fine, *a mhaistir,*" and we sat facing each other across the litter of the table, his a plain wooden chair, mine of tubular steel, sprayed hospital green.

"I hate to have to go into this, *a mhaistir.* You've always been a good teacher. You've always pulled your weight with the team here, but Father Curry has asked me to," he began, using that ingratiating tone of the country when it is uncomfortable. "It's come to his notice that you are living as a married man, when in fact you don't appear to be married."

"I am married."

"You're still on the single scale. You've never obtained a letter of freedom."

"I married in a registry office during the year's leave of absence I had."

"Father Curry guessed as much. What possessed you to do it, *a mhaistir*? I've always found you reasonable and sensible. Some people fly off the handle and you can't reason with them but I've never found you that way," he put his head in his hands.

"It wasn't possible to be married in the church. My wife was married before."

"I don't know why it should happen this way. Life should be simpler, but you must know, *a mhaistir*, you won't be allowed to continue teaching in a Catholic school?"

I was silent and then he asked, "What do you intend to do, *a mhaistir*?" and when I shrugged he said, "I strongly advise you, *a mhaistir*, that the best thing for you to do is just to resign."

Cut your own throat. Don't rock the boat. A great man. When he had to face up to it he did the decent. A decent man. He faced up to his mistake. He caused no one trouble.

"I won't resign, *a mhaistir*."

"Why, *a mhaistir?* You must know I've discussed this with Father Curry already. If you don't resign you'll be dismissed. Why bring it to that, *a mhaistir?*"

"I've thought about it too, *a mhaistir*, and I won't resign. If I was a lousy teacher I'd resign or had committed some crime or had harmed a child it'd be different. But I'm harming no one."

"But how, *a mhaistir*, can you stand before a class and teach Catechism?"

"While living in sin?" I put it for him and he dumbly nodded his head back into his hands. "That's no trouble, *a mhaistir*. You know that as well as I do. All you need to teach is knowledge and skill. If I refused to teach it on a point of principle then I'd have to resign but I don't refuse. It's written down in black and white in the official *Notes For Teachers* on history that the cultivation of patriotism is more important than truth. So when we teach history Britain is always the big black beast, Ireland is the poor daughter struggling while being raped, when most of us know it's a lot more complicated than that. And yet we teach it."

"I know, I know, *a mhaistir*, but this is different. There are Managers who wouldn't allow you to continue teaching even if you married a Protestant girl within the church."

"That's their business. I won't resign." We both rose.

"I'll have to tell Father Curry this but you know the result will be the same," he said as he showed me to the door. I was silent and he put an affectionate hand on my shoulder, "Ah, *a mhaistir*, why had things to get like this? Life should be simple. Little did we think it would come to this as we had those bottles of lemonade that Sunday you were first appointed. I thought you'd have long and happy years at the school that Sunday."

I was met by tension everywhere I went, on the concrete, in the corridor, the lunchroom, but nothing was spoken in my presence. That was two days ago, and first thing yesterday the quiet James knocked on my door, "The *Priomh-oide* wants to see you in the office. He asked me to take over the class till you get back," he was embarrassed and kept his eyes averted towards some writing on the blackboard. "That's fine. They're just at the Catechism around the Eucharist."

He was waiting for me in the office and rose affably, "*Tog cathaoir, a mhaistir*," and I took the tubular steel chair.

"I saw Father Curry and he's still prepared to accept your resignation. You'll have no trouble, with your degrees, getting a much better position than you can ever hope for here, in England. And if you resign I can give you a glowing reference in good conscience. In fact, your teaching and qualifications deserve no less," he said and waited nervously.

"It's no use, *a mhaistir*. I won't resign," and I saw him harden himself into a steely formality, the robes and black hat of the judge, garbing him in his function. He is no longer a dying person pronouncing premature death on a fellow but an abstraction.

"Then, *a mhaistir*, I have to inform you that from the end of this week, tomorrow, you can no longer teach here."

"I mean no rudeness, *a mhaistir*, but you have no authority to dismiss me. That's the Manager's job. They are having others do their dirty work for them for too long. The only form of dismissal I'll accept is from the Manager, either in writing or in person," and he went very red. I was sorry for him.

"I'll have to contact the Manager again, *a mhaistir*," he stammered. I heard him dialling as I went down the corridor to take back the class from James. An hour or so later a boy knocked on the door with a note: it was from the headmaster. *The Manager will see you at eight tomorrow evening.* Good man, I thought, put nothing in writing in case there's trouble as I scribbled *Will be there at eight* at the foot of the note handed it back to the waiting boy.

I look at my watch where I stare from the counter out on the rain and hazy bay. It will be that eight in three hours. It is time to go to meet Lightfoot in the Stag's Head. It looks settled for an evening and night of rain.

I find Lightfoot already seated on a highstool at the counter of the Stag's Head, a book between his elbows on the marble, a half-finished pint of stout; the slender stem of the clock rises from the marble, the beautiful Roman numerals of the white face encased with silver, crowned with the silver antlers. "Beware of the high stool. A teacher has too many hours to kill," they had said as I left to train.

"I seem to read nothing these days except history. A sign of laziness, but it stays still. *It* at least is settled. What are you having?" he asks as he closes the book. I ask for a soda water.

"That's an unusual order," he comments as he beckons to one of the white-aproned barmen.

"I have to meet this priest at eight. I'm being fired from the school. There's no use risking handing out an unnecessary advantage and I want to see it fully through. I've always been in entire sympathy with the French gentleman who asked to be guillotined face up so that he could see the blade come down."

"I knew there was something up when you rang but at least you foresaw that it would happen sooner or later," he says and I tell him the story of the last few days.

"It's extraordinary but not surprising to anybody who knows this crazy country," he says when I finish. "Will you try to get the Union to take it up or anything?"

"No. If it was some sort of inefficiency they'd probably fight but not on such a private matter of faith or morals. They'd not confront the Church in light years on such a delicate matter."

"At least you're married in law. You could take it to the courts."

"That's not even certain. There's the special relationship the Church has. . ."

"I'd forgotten about that completely," and he groped for the year the statute was brought in.

"I haven't the money anyhow, and, more important, look at the waste of time and life it'd be. It'd not be worth it."

"I'm afraid I'd take your view but it's an uneasy business. There's the boredom and risk and waste and yet it seems a duty: injustice should be opposed at almost any cost. I think all that will one day change naturally. Soon it will be impossible to take away a person's living just because he can't get married the way you want him to. I came on an extraordinary story recently. Though it has nothing much to do with what we've been talking about," he changes as I order the second round. It'll be some time, I think, before I look on the warm varnished wood of the great barrels on the shelves in the evening again, their metal hoops and copper taps on which the pewter measures hang.

"There was this boxer," he names a famous amateur of not so many years back. "He had the misfortune to fall calamitously in love with this woman. And do you know what he went and did?—you'd think it'd take a great poet to imagine it! He had all his trophies, gold and silver, cups and medals and statues, melted down and shaped into ornaments for the woman—bangles, pendants, earrings, necklaces, even a wedding ring made from his European Gold Medal—and she threw him over only to discover soon that such passions couldn't be inspired everyday of the week, and didn't she come back and marry him two years later. The story has been fascinating me," he laughs in ironic wonderment as he drinks.

"Did he have the ornaments themselves when she did come back?"

"I don't know," he laughs. "Apparently he's now just an ordinary fellow going bald and running into fat, with a couple of kids, pushing a lawnmower on some suburban lawn on summer evenings."

I would love to stay but the hands of the silver clock have long passed seven. "I have to go but why don't you stay?"

"I think I will stay. I'll read and probably have another drink. I don't particularly want to go home yet. What'll you do though after tonight?"

"We'll go back to London."

"When?"

"Probably tomorrow on the nightboat. There's no use hanging round once it is over. We don't have much to pack."

"Why don't you let me pick you up in the car and we can all have dinner together before you get on the boat."

I thank him as I leave and say, "I'll ring in the morning when I'm certain," and think, old friend who loathes friendship, I'll miss you when I leave.

A path between privet, a lion's claw of brass, and behind the halfopened door the priest's housekeeper, her suspicious face.

"Oh it's you. He's waiting for you."

I follow her up a dark hallway. She knocks, "Your visitor, Father," and steals me a venomous glance as she withdraws; they say she makes all his important decisions for him.

Slowly he places the missal he has been reading on the mantel, its pagemarkers hang over the edge, delicate ribbons of red and black and gold and green and blue and brown. A single bar of an electric fire glows between his legs. We shake hands.

"I hope you didn't get wet."

"No, but it's a wet night, Father."

He motions me towards a facing armchair, the tin back of the electric fire toward me, I can see the red glow of the bar on his black cloth.

"So you won't resign?"

"No, Father."

"Well, don't you know that leaves me no option but to get rid of you?"

"Why, Father?"

"You know that better than I do. If it got out that I let you go on teaching up there after what you've gone and done there'd be an uproar. The Archbishop wouldn't stand for it. The parents wouldn't stand for it. I couldn't stand for it." I notice there's a strong smell of whiskey in the room. "Tell me this one fact. What entered your head to do such a thing? Didn't you know it was flying in the face of God? You never caused me any trouble. I thought you'd see my days out at the school. Now you go and leave me no option but to get rid of you. Tell me this, what entered your head to do it?"

So this farce is another of the deaths.

"I met someone I wanted to marry. There was no other way to do it."

"God, I always thought you were steady enough. Isn't there thousands of Irish Catholic girls crying out for a husband? Why couldn't you go and marry one of them?"

"You're dismissing me then, Father?"

"Shure, you left me with no option, but it'd be simpler if you'd resign."

"I won't resign, Father."

"You leave me with no option then," he rises from the chair, his shoe knocking against the heater, and goes to the bureau in the corner of the room. He takes and hands me an envelope. I open it and read the single typed sentence formally dismissing me from the school.

"Would you have a drop of whiskey?" he offers.

"Thanks, Father."

He takes a bottle of whiskey and two glasses from the same bureau and pours two large measures. He hands me a glass and takes his seat again in front of the electric bar.

"Does the whiskey trouble your ulcer at all, Father?" I resume my role on the concrete, a glass of whiskey instead of the tongue of the bell in my hand.

"The doctors tell you not to touch it but if you did everything the doctors told you to do your life wouldn't be worth living."

"You should be going on your holidays soon, Father."

"Next week. If you didn't get a break from this parish and its troubles off and on you'd go off your head."

"Will you go to Rome this year?"

"No. I find it too depressing. All my old friends are either buried there or transferred to the corners of the earth. Last year for the first time I couldn't bring myself to attend the reunion in the Gresham. I'll go down the country."

"Will you stay in hotels or with friends."

"In hotels of course. You might as well stay at home if you have to stay with friends. You have to fit in with their ways of going about. It's all right to call on them for an hour or two as long as you have the hotel to go back to. The worst of the hotels is that central heating. Suffocating. They all went wild on it with the subsidies they got from Bord Failte."

I look over the old fat priest in his overcoat in the chair, the red electric bar between his legs—this is what she had dreamed for me—and I shiver.

"Well, what do you intend to do now?" his bluffness does not hide his unease. I finish the last of the whiskey and wonder if the condemned had not sometimes to help the part-time hangmen with rope and trapdoor.

"I'll go to London, Father."

"It's a vastly overcrowded place to my way of thinking."

As I grow older I feel great cities give more freedom than ever the mountains did but I answer, "It's not difficult to find work there."

"If there's a reference or anything I can do for you there just write to me. You never caused me no trouble. What I can't understand is what entered your head to do what you have done," he pauses, tired and heavy and old in the swaddling of his greatcoat.

"Do you think if the marriage could be put right in the eyes of the church that I'd be allowed to teach in this country again?" I probe as much out of curiosity as out of some old fear I feel in the face of the finality of the dismissal and I see him pause to think.

"I doubt it. Hardly in my time. You see, once any authority makes a judgement it takes an even greater authority to reverse the decision. I can't see that happening in our time."

"The Archbishop?" I ask.

"Don't you know the Archbishop knows all about your case, child!"

"I was fairly certain."

"What I do advise you to do though is that as soon as you get yourself settled in London to go along to your Parish Priest and for your own peace of mind discuss with him if there's any way the marriage can be made holy."

We both rise. As he offers me his hand he puts his other hand on my shoulder. "I'll remember you in my prayers. Say a prayer for me sometime too."

"Goodbye, Father."

"God be with you."

In the rain of the street I finger the letter I forced them to give me and wonder was it worth it, and the answer that comes is probably not, and then I think the same answer belongs to all of life. To my disturbance I have to fight back emotion. I hear the beating apart of the iron beds with the priest by her head on the pillow. In the laurels I follow her coffin on the last journey and think of her dreams for me. Dressed in scarlet and white I pour wine and water into the chalice in the priest's hands on the altar. In scarlet and white I attend at the mysteries of Holy Week to the triumphant clamour of the Easter bells. I see the priest addressing us again as we prepared to leave the Training College, trained to teach the young, the Second Priesthood, and this evening it all seems strewn about my life as waste, and it too had belonged once in rude confidence to a day.

My love waits for me in a room at Howth. The table will have bread and meat and cheap wine and flowers. Tomorrow we will go on the boat to London. It will be neither a return or a departure but a continuing. We will be true to another and to our separate selves and each day we will renew it again and again and again. It is the only communion left to us now. Oh soul full of grace, pray for me, now and at the hour, Oh pray for us both; even now I feel the desperate need of prayer. But use your head for Christ's sake, I start to think, and I master myself and stand out of the rain in the doorway of a shop to wait for the bus to Howth.

I get off at the stop past Howth Station to walk a few minutes by the harbour. Some boats of the fishing fleet are moored to the wall, their wet decks gleam under the glare of the harbour lights, nets and coils of rope and winches and empty fish boxes. A fisherman comes out of his cabin into the white glare and empties a teapot over the side and only a door creaks as he silently returns to the mystery of the dimly lighted cabin, above it the still wings of the radar. The full tide surges against the wall and boats, withdraws, and surges back. "Begin and cease, and then again begin." It was Matthew Arnold. And ... "it brought into his mind the turbid ebb and flow of human misery." That bright girdle he spoke of had been long broken for me too before this last night. I turn uphill from the sea and boats towards the room. There are no lights on downstairs. The Logans had gone visiting or early to bed. A line of yellow is drawn beneath the door of the room.

She is waiting for me. Her hair is damp as we kiss.

"I went out. Somehow I got nervous around eight. I knew that was the time you had the meeting and I went for a walk along the shore. Look what I found," she hands me a white stone, oblong and round and completely smoothed, blue veins running through the stone, cold and soothing to the hands. Always she brings these stones and shells from the shore. A child? Rounded and full the lovely body of a woman, shaped for luxury and sorrow; a man's angular body, made for work and strife.

"Here. This is all I could get out of them," I show her the formal sentence of dismissal. "At least its gone through with. I felt sorry though for the poor bugger of a priest. He had just to do his job when it came to the crunch. It was unpleasant for him, and he was embarrassed."

"Did you learn anything new?"

"No. Nothing. It was all as I told you it would be."

"When will we leave then?" she asks quietly.

"We might as well leave tomorrow night if we can manage the packing. There's no use hanging round now."

"A few hours will finish the packing."

"Lightfoot says he'll call and take the cases to the boat. He wants us to have dinner together before we leave."

"We couldn't leave a nicer way than that."

We are not departing. We are continuing. She lights a single white candle standing in an ashtray on the table. I watch its wavering flower of flame on the two wine glasses when she turns out the light, "Do you mind drawing the cork?" How vulnerable the slender nape of the neck is as she ladles out kidneys and steaming rice. The rough red wine is sour but its alcohol loosens our tongues: the first constant was water, the gull's shadow floats again on the concrete, tea leaves are emptied into the tide, another day of our lives is almost ended, Ah, love, let us be true to one another! When we tire we hear the rain on the slates and in the distance the muffled breathing of the sea.

"Will we go for a last turn on the front or will we go to bed?"

"I think I'd rather go to bed."

The candle is blown out. I wait for her between cool linen. Her slender white arms glimmer above her head in the darkness. I hear the soft brittle rustle of underclothes falling free on to the back of the chair. The boat has slipped its moorings and is leaving harbour to trust to the open sea: and no boat needs so much trust to put to sea as it does for one body to go human and naked and vulnerable into the arms of another.

We have grown so used to one another that our loving is like breathing and when she cries out to me the lingering fire of our loving breaks into a last flame, and then such stillness comes that all sounds are clear, the rain on the roof, the distant sea, our close breathing.

"What are you thinking, love?"

"Nothing much. Something quite silly in fact. I was thinking that if I happen to conceive tonight it would be a very quiet child."

The odour of our lovemaking rises, redolent of slime and fish, and our very breathing seems an echo of the rise and fall of the sea as we drift to sleep; and I would pray for the boat of our sleep to reach its morning, and see that morning lengthen to an evening of calm weather that comes through night and sleep again to morning after morning until we meet the first death.